Northern Lights

<u>Books and Stories by Ron Mueller</u>
<u>The Taelo Series</u>
Taelo: The Early Years
Taelo: The Golden Feather
Taelo: Journey of Discovery
Taelo: Dangerous Passage
Taelo: Condor Clan Slingers
Taelo: Circumvention
Taelo: The Journey of Sages
Taelo: Collection
Taelo: Future Leaders Journey

<u>A Taelo Story:</u>
White Swan and Quiet Pheasant
The Child's Name
Floating Cloud
Quiet Rabbit
Busy Bee
Little Otter & Talking Wren
Broken Spear
Burley Bear & Meadow Flower

<u>Science Fiction</u>
The Savitar Series:
    Journey's End
    Savitar
    Confluence

Bram Nielson Series
    The Fold
    The Message
    Fold Wormhole
    Negative Fold
    Ripples in Time

<u>Single Science Fiction Books:</u>
    Current Past and Future
    The Event
    The Door
    Viajante 7

Ron Mueller

<u>Fiction Series</u>

The Alex Evercrest Series
    The River Front
    The Girl on The Grill
    Missing
    Maggot
    Racist
    Votive Candles
    Windy City
    Country Road
    Pool of Blood
    Sins of the Daughter
    Body Parts
    The Skull Collector
    The Vanishing
    The Shadow Fighter
    Moonshine
    Grief's Trajectory
    The Magic Touch
    Northern Lights

A Brian Oneil Novell
    Hawaiian Phoenix
    Moon Curser
    Death Broker

The Problem Solver Series
    Solutions
    Drug Lords
    Border Crosser

Imagination by Courtney Huynh and Chloe Parker

Northern Lights

Northern Lights
By: *Ron Mueller*

Around the World Publishing LLC
4914 Cooper Road Suite 144
Cincinnati, Ohio 45242-9998

This story is a work of fiction. Names, characters, places, and incidents either are products of the author's imagination or are used fictitiously. Any resemblance to actual events or locales or persons, living or dead, is entirely coincidental.

ISBN 13: 978-1-68223-960-5
ISBN 10: 1-68223-960-8

Distributed by Ingram
Alex Evercrest Model By: Pi03@ShutterStock
Cover Picture by: Nataliia Korzhenevska @ShutterStock
Cover by: Ron Mueller

Ron Mueller

Northern Lights

<u>Table of Content</u>

Ron Mueller

Northern Lights

<u>**Chapter 1: Twelve Barrels**</u>

Grayson unhooked his oil line from the pipeline, came down the ladder with the capped oil line. He slipped the line into its tube mount on the frame above the oil barrels. He put the ladder alongside of the tube and strapped it in place. He made sure all twelve barrels had their fill and vent openings tightly secured. This was the exact process that he had practiced for the past ten years.

He took the oil from the pipeline, transported it to Valdez and sold it to his contact, Miles Walker, who worked for an oil company but had his own side hustle buying oil from small oil producers.

He made two trips a week and sold twelve barrels each time. Miles provided him with twelve empty barrels and paid him sixty percent of the current market price for oil. He wondered where Miles got his empty barrels, but he never asked. He took them, filled them, and returned them.

Ron Mueller

For the last ten years since he had quit working on the pipeline as a welder he had made his living by tapping into the pipeline in several locations where he had installed the taps before he had quit working on the line. The taps were inconspicuous and did not show up on any of the pipeline drawings.

He was his own boss, had plenty of time off and was making around ninety grand a year. It took him about ten minutes per barrel or two hours to fill all twelve barrels. Thirty minutes to set up and the put away his line and ladder. And then there was the drive to Valdez that ate up sixteen hours each way three times a week. So, in total he spent about sixty working hours a week, made eighteen hundred dollars or around ninety grand a year. That put him at the top of the money-making ladder. He felt really good about that.

Often after one of his trips he would go out to celebrate another successful run by splurging on a nice dinner and enjoying a few drinks. That periodically included going out with the one of the few available women that resided in Valdez or Fairbanks.

At first he had just stayed at a bed and breakfast but then he had purchased a home. He spent about two thirds of his time at his house and during the summer weather he would walk around the track that surrounded the Valdez High School football field or go fishing in the harbor. He felt that he had successfully set himself up for life.

Northern Lights

He was well known at the five hotels in Prudhoe Bay and Deadhorse where he had stayed if the weather kept him from making the trip back to Valdez. He hated to do it because it meant that he had to keep his truck running the whole time so he would not risk ruining his engine due to the cold. He learned that timing the filling of his barrels and then getting on the road was a critical factor. He followed a strict routine and usually got home before bad weather kept him out.

Then one day he climbed the ladder to his oil tap line and found that someone had sealed it so that he could not open it. He could figure out how to open the valve safely without the risk of breaking the line and creating an oil spill. He decided that he needed to find out who had sealed the valve and he needed to eliminate that individual or else his he faced the certainty of having to work for some company once again for a pittance. He felt that his future was at risk, and he was not going to accept that risk without a fight.

He found a high point where he had a good view of the above ground part of the pipeline. His taps were spread along the four hundred twenty miles that were above ground. The specific locations were determined by the fact that he could reach them with his ladder and have his truck close enough that his hose could reach all of the twelve barrels. That meant that most of his taps were closer to Prudhoe Bay area or in the few spots that were farther south. He had a few others that were harder to get to, so they were seldom used.

Ron Mueller

For several trips he would slowly drive along Dalton Highway and follow the pipeline. He was trying to find who might have discovered his taps. He was aware that each of the large oil companies had inspection teams that drove the pipeline to make sure that there were no leaks. That inspection happened every day and took in all four hundred twenty miles of the above ground pipe. His taps were on the opposite side of the pipe of where the inspectors drove so they could not be visually seen from the road. He was looking for someone who was looking from the tap side of the line.

It took him almost six months to finally see someone walking on that side of the pipe. He stopped his truck, took out his rifle and looked through the scope at the person. It was clear to him that he was an Inuit. They had fought for years to block the pipeline but had lost to the money handlers who had bought off the Inuit leaders as well as all the Alaskan politicians. The money had talked, and the pipeline went in.

He had no idea who this individual happened to be.

He watched as the individual stopped at a point where one of his taps was located. In this area he always filled the oil in the dark of night. He knew that he needed to take action because he could not afford to lose any more taps, especially taps in the easy to access areas.

He looked around to make sure there was no one on the road, or with in site and made his decision.

Northern Lights

He looked through his scope put the cross hairs on the person's chest and pulled the trigger. It should have been a kill shot but his target had at the last moment bent over to pick something up from the ground and the shot had hit him, knocked him down but he saw the person crawl away.

He jumped off the truck and ran toward the pipeline. When he got there, he was surprised to find nothing.

He looked along the creek and again he saw nothing. He looked for a trail of blood and found nothing. He knew that he had not missed but he found nothing. He walked along the creek looking for any sign. He finally gave up and returned to his truck. He picked up the single casing from the back of the truck bed and put his rifle back on the rack and strapped it in. He drove about ten miles to where he had another tap, filled his oil barrels, and then drove on toward Valdez. He knew he had to return as soon as he could and set himself up to shoot anyone else that might show up.

Ignirtoq looked along the pipeline that he had walked multiple times from one end to the other. He had walked the many miles of exposed piping and he had walked over the miles where the pipeline was buried. He understood that it was purposely built to have a zig-zag pattern in case of a significant earthquake. He had been a young boy when the plans to build the pipeline had been made public and had participated with his Inuit brethren that objected to having it built.

Ron Mueller

Money ended up winning. The state and federal government politicians were influenced by the desire for the oil money and succumbed to the allure of the tax income, the royalty income, and the promises of other improvements. The North Slope Borough representing the Inuit was allotted enough shares of stock that they were convinced to approve the pipeline and were now getting six hundred million a year in dividends and had become the wealthiest company in Alaska.

Ignirtoq had come to accept the pipeline and the fact that his people as well at the other indigenous people had also benefitted. He had taken advantage of the situation and had attended University of Alaska Fairbanks and had majored in forestry. He had stayed in the university to earn a graduate interdisciplinary degree that spanned across mechanical engineering, linguistics of the region, and tribal governance. His resume and his Inuit heritage made him an attractive hire to the oil companies.

He was hired by one of the big oil firms and went to work for them after his graduation. He had accepted the role as a technical inspector of the oil line and became familiar with every above and below ground mile of the line. He worked for more than ten years and rose to a mid-level manager.

His life in his community took on a political slant and he was elected a local tribal leader. He saved almost his entire income and when he quit the oil company to pursue other avenues, he knew that he had enough to live comfortably.

Northern Lights

It was at this point that he got married to the young woman who he had met while at the university. They had only one child a son, Kaskae who after his wife died of lung cancer, he raised on his own. The two of them were close and they still lived together. They had hunted and fished together, and he had taught him all the ways of surviving in the Iñupiaq Region. He had shown him how to survive where the ground could not support large trees and he had taken him to the mountains where the snow depth often would reach more than twenty feet. There he had taught him how to shuffle through the snow on large snowshoes and to build a shelter using the snow and then being able to sit inside where a large candle would provide enough heat to allow them to sit in, take off their coats and be comfortable in their thermal underwear.

All of this was going through his mind as he closed the opening to the crevasse at the edge of the stream. He needed time to assess how badly he was hurt, and he had to make sure that the person who had shot him could not find him. He had his own weapon, but he needed to recover before exiting and making his way back to his all-terrain snowmobile scooter that he had left not more than a mile away hidden in under some brush.

Ron Mueller

Kaskae had been expecting his father home. He knew that his father was most likely on one of his many inspection tours of the oil pipeline and perhaps had forgotten the time. If he had planned to be out for more than a day, he would have let everyone know. There was no word from him, and he did not show up to dinner.

He called his cousin Atiqtalik, who was a local forest ranger, to see if she had heard anything only to learn that she had not. She shared that his father had let her know that there was someone stealing oil from the pipeline. He didn't care about the thievery, but he was worried that the thief might create an oil spill.

Kaskae asked how anyone could possibly tap into the pipeline since it operated at a very high pressure.

Atiqtalik said that she had wondered the same thing and had asked his father who explained that the taps would have had to be put in during the construction of the pipeline and since they had not been noticed then they would have been put in by someone working during the construction of the pipeline and be installed in such a fashion that the tap would blend in with the other equipment that might be part of the various pipe joints.

Northern Lights

She added that she and her team had been stumped and had reported the possibility of someone selling stolen oil. She had been informed that there were several sellers of small quantities of oil by the barrel that fit the profile but most of them did have their own small oil wells and it would take some time to check them all out.

She said that she would get her unit to go along the pipeline and see what they could find.

A few days later she replied that she had found the all-terrain snowmobile hidden in the brush. She had left it in place just in case her uncle came back he would have it if he needed it.

Grayson returned to the area where he suspected the person he had shot should be. He again checked everywhere and after spending more time than he wished he decided to take his oil to Valdez. He had used up a full day in hopes of finding the person he had shot and who he knew he had hit. It puzzled him how that person could disappear in an area that had no place to hide.

He decided that he would next use one of the taps that was farther south and stay away from the area where this mysterious person had appeared. He continued to be worried about the fact that the person had somehow been able to identify the oil tap. It was well enough disguised that it had never been noticed by anyone inspecting the line. Whoever the person was they had to know a lot about the pipeline to have found the tap.

He decided that he would curtail his oil runs and return and focus his efforts on finding and eliminating anyone looking for the taps. He felt he had to protect his investment.

Ignirtoq assessed his wound and decided that it was superficial. He thought about the situation and decided that everyone needed to think he had been killed. He needed to be dead so that he could get the person who he knew would solve the mystery of who was stealing the oil, and she would only come if he was thought of as dead. He had been impressed with her ability to solve cases that others failed to.

He sent his brother a cryptic message that he had been shot, was dying and that he should contact an Alex Evercrest, in Cincinnati, Ohio and see if she could be hired to solve who had killed him.

He figured it was a long shot, but he had enough food and water that he could last for several weeks, and he had a fishing line that he could throw into the stream below to catch a few trout.

Atiqtalik learned of the call that her father had received. She looked up the person who her uncle had called out by name and was impressed by what she learned. She wondered when her uncle had learned about her, but she decided she would make the call to see if she would take on the case. She decided to go through the official organization channels. She wanted to make sure that she got a positive response to getting this "Alex" involved in a case that was taking a very weird twist.

Northern Lights

She had the tribal leaders to deal with. She was a forest ranger and not a criminal law enforcer. She wanted the help if she could get it.

She asked Kaskae if he had the money to pay for such a venture.

He said that he was on his father's bank account and there was more than enough money available if she thought involving a Qallunaat would do any good.

Atiqtalik laughed and said that the person she was getting involved was not a Qallunaat but was black.

That caught him by surprise. He asked why she was asking for her. She replied that she had a reputation for solving cases that no one else could and that his father had somehow zeroed in on her.

Kaskae said that if his father had specifically called this detective out then he had to support getting her to Alaska.

Grayson returned from Valdez to the location where he had made the shot that he knew had hit the person he had aimed for. He came prepared to stay and wait for his quarry to show himself. He did not plan to set up a camp, but he had a portable one-person hutch that he could sit comfortably in, stay warm and enjoy his coffee. He figured it was just like a hunting trip, but he was hunting a very specific two-legged game. He found a location where the hutch camouflage disappeared into the background.

Ron Mueller

He laughed as he thought about the well-known saying, "there is a woman behind every tree." It was a joke about the fact that there were so few women in this northern region and no trees that anyone could hide behind. In this case he was the shooter that was waiting behind those same trees.

He would wait until he either saw the person who had somehow hidden from him or saw his body hauled away.

Northern Lights

Chapter 2: A call out of the Blue

The Chief listened to the person on the other end as she explained the reason that he should grant the request to have Alex help to solve a potential murder case that involved her grand uncle. The details seemed to be sketchy and not clear to him and he was skeptical of taking the case on since it was in northern Alaska along the oil pipeline. He wondered whether Alex would even be interested in taking on such a case.

He asked the person on the phone to hold on for a moment. He went to the door and signaled Alex and Trey to come to his office.

They entered and he briefly explained the call and then put the call into speaker mode and let the caller know that he had called Alex and her partner into his office to listen to her request.

Atiqtalik introduced herself and shared the fact that she was a forest ranger in the northern part of Alaska and lived in Wiseman which was just east of Gates of the Arctic National Park and Preserve. She chuckled and asked if either of them had a clue where she was located.

Alex laughed and said that she certainly would need to look on the map of Alaska to have a clue. She went on to ask why she was being asked to investigate a potential murder.

Atiqtalik replied that her grand uncle had disappeared, but he had contacted his brother, her father and let him know that he had been shot but hoped to recover but if he did not return in a day or two that his brother should call in Alex Evercrest to find the person who had killed him.

Alex asked if her grand uncle's body had been found.

Atiqtalik was silent for a moment and then she said that it had not. She had found his all-terrain snow scooter hidden in low spot under some brush along the oil pipeline. She went on to explain that her grand uncle constantly patrolled the pipeline to ensure there were no leaks. He had recently become convinced that someone was stealing oil from the pipeline, and he was trying to find out who and how that was being done. He was sure that such activity would lead to a major spill.

Alex looked at the Chief and asked if he had the funds to let her, and Trey do an initial investigation to determine if there was a case.

Atiqtalik spoke up and said that she was prepared to cover the cost of that initial investigation and any additional cost if Alex took up the case.

Northern Lights

Alex said that the initial investigation would be having her, and her partner come to the location that was specified. So, the expenses would be to get there, get a hotel room and then have some sort of transportation.

Atiqtalik replied that she would cover that but if it became a longer-term case, she was not sure how that would be handled.

Alex suggested that they should take it one step at a time.

Atiqtalik suggested they fly into Prospect Creek, and she would meet them there with her partner and take them to the hotel were they could stay.

After the call Alex looked over at the Chief and commented that this was very different than the start of some of the other cases.

He laughed and said that he no longer evaluated how her cases did or did not start. He agreed that it was different than being shot at on her bike ride into work, or having a child dropped off on her porch, but it was similar to getting a call from the Royal Canadian Mounted Police and asking her to help them on a case that turned out as a hunt for a serial killer black widow.

Alex looked at Trey and asked if he could leave the following day.

Trey nodded and said that he and Lindsey did not have any plans.

She let the Chief know that she was going to get his support associate to arrange the flight to Prospect Creek, Alaska.

The Chief laughed and asked what the population was at Prospect Creek happened to be and how large the plane taking her there was going to be.

Alex shook her head and said she had no idea how to answer either of his questions. She added that she knew that Fairbanks Alaska was ten percent the size of Cincinnati and that Fairbanks was around thirty thousand, so she figured that Prospect Creek was really small. She then added that they would most likely be flying in into Prospect Creek on a piper cub and both of them might have to peddled to provide the power for the plane.

She estimated that they would be gone for a week unless they actually had a case to open then she would talk with him to determine what to do next.

The Chief nodded and wished her a good trip.

She left the office and shared what had just happened with Johnnie, Bill, and Trevor.

Trevor looked at her and joked that she was probably using the trip as an excuse to go skiing and she was leaving those who were serious about doing actual work behind.

Alex said that as far as she knew she would be on some of the flattest terrain in Alaska and looking up at an eight-foot diameter oil pipeline. But if she found some good skiing she would make sure to give him a call.

She looked at Johnnie and let him know that she was riding home and that he was welcome to ride with her.

Northern Lights

Trey said that he was going home as well and would pack for Alaska. He asked about the weather.

Bill said that it was the time of year when it would be very cold in the northern part of Alaska and long underwear would be appropriate.

On the ride home, Alex chatted with Johnnie and asked whether Mary might be able to spend a few more hours taking care of Aurea and making sure that Matt had some help in the evenings and early morning.

Johnnie replied that he was sure that Mary would be able to do that. He suggested that once they got to her house, she talk with Mary so that the two of them were clear on what was wanted.

She got home just before Mary and Aurea came home from school. They came in the back door because the two of them were still able to ride their bikes and the street behind the house was at the same level that they rode from the house to the school.

Aurea was surprised to have Alex home early and asked what was up.

Alex explained about the call and the trip she was going to make.

Aurea surprised everyone by commenting that Prudhoe Bay was the farthest north location in Alaska, it was where all the oil wells were located and that the coldest part of the year was just starting. She added that all of Alaska had less than half population of the greater Cincinnati area.

Alex complemented Aurea for knowing so much about Alaska.

Aurea said that was one of the places she had visited online. She was fascinated by the fact that the oil pipeline was so big and traveled across a great deal of the state to a location where ships and trucks could be loaded year-round to move the oil to market. She went on to explain that it represented about twenty percent of the oil produced by the United States.

Mary said that it was time for the two of them to go to the library to their first seminar and she wanted to get there early enough so the two of them did not miss out on any of the refreshments. She took Aurea the hand and said that their cab was waiting. She made sure Aurea had her homework with her so that it would get done before they came back for dinner.

Alex spent a few moments with Johnnie after the two of them left. She clarified that she was planning to get him involved if she needed any specific information.

Johnnie nodded and added that cookies were still the currency of choice for any specific requests that required his magic touch.

Alex laughed, went to the cupboard, and took out a container full of cookies and said that she was paying in advance because she didn't want to be stuck in ten feet of snow and not be able to get his help.

She then said that she had to get her things packed for the trip.

Northern Lights

She packed both her thermal underwear, her full Kevlar suit and all the winter clothes she thought might come in handy. She managed to get all of it into one large hard-shelled suitcase. She had a second smaller case as a carryon for her computer and paperwork.

She had just finished when Matt came in, looked at the still open suitcase and commented that he was glad that he had come home before she ran away.

Alex laughed and said that she had just finished packing for a trip to the North Pole and planned to visit Santa and ask him personally for what she wanted for Christmas. She gave him a hug and then went down to the kitchen and said that she was going to start dinner.

She got him a snack and then let him know that she was going to Alaska to investigate a potential murder.

Matt listened and said that it sounded like a potentially dangerous investigation.

Alex nodded and said that she was going to be as safe as possible but as always, she would approach it as if someone was trying to shoot her.

Dinner was ready when Mary returned with Aurea from the library.

Mary excused herself and said that she and Johnnie had agreed to go to dinner and then take a walk around Hyde Park.

After dinner, the three of them spent a quiet evening chatting and reading in the family room.

Ron Mueller

Matt left to meet his EMT team at four in the morning. He quietly wished Alex a safe journey and went out to his team who had come by to pick him up.

Alex got up and made breakfast for her and Aurea.

Mary came in as the two of them were just finishing cleaning off the table and putting the dishes in the dishwasher.

Aurea gave Alex a hug and asked her to call and to send pictures.

Alex said that she would do that every day.

After Mary and Aurea left, Alex took her suitcases to the street in back, got into the cab and headed to the Airport.

She met Trey and the two of them went to the counter and checked in. They checked their luggage through to Fairbanks where they were to be met by Clay who would fly them on a Piper PA-18 Super Cub chartered by the U.S. Fish and Wildlife Service. He explained that Atiqtalik had arranged for him to fly the two of them to Bettles, which was a change to the where she had previously said would be the final destination.

He explained that the new location was closer to where they would be staying and would save them a lot of time.

He led them out to a white van and got their suitcases in the back and had them sit on the bench seats behind him. He drove out to the cub.

Alex noticed what to her were extremely large tires on such a small plane. She asked about the size of the tires.

Northern Lights

He laughed and said that they were twenty six-inch Alaskan Bushwheels and cost close to two thousand dollars each. He used them because they were tough, and they let him land on almost any surface.

Alex looked at Trey and said that the planes were getting smaller, the tires were getting larger but at least they didn't have to peddle but would still be flying first class.

Clay smiled and said that he was pleased that she thought the flight would be first class and he assured her that she would not have to peddle. He pointed to a cooler with refreshment that they could enjoy on their first-class flight.

Alex was surprised at the smooth take off, the fact that the inside of the plane was not as loud as she had expected and that the view of the terrain was constantly changing from a thick dark green pine cover with a few broad leaf trees to a more rugged terrain where the trees diminished and by the time they reached Bettles both the number of trees and their size had both greatly diminished. In fact, it appeared as if the trees were huddling along various small streams and there were vast distanced between the huddling trees.

Clay brought the P18 cub to a smooth landing and guided it back to where two people were standing by a white SUV with blue and red flashing lights on the top and a green strip from the headlights running just below the side windows to the backlights.

Clay let them know that the one that looked like a forest ranger was Atiqtalik and the stout stocky guy was Kaskae her cousin. He added that Atiqtalik was the one that had made the arrangements with him. He was aware that Kaskae's father, Ignirtoq was missing, and that Alex had been asked to investigate his disappearance.

Alex asked why he said that Ignirtoq was missing.

Clay smiled and said that Ignirtoq was too stubborn to have been killed. He added that Ignirtoq was a master of the terrain, knew how to survive in the most terrible conditions of weather and through the most difficult of situations. Clay said that his money was on the fact that he had wanted her to come to Alaska to solve some problem that he had not been able to solve and that his death was the only way to get her to come.

Alex laughed and said that she was going to keep his words in mind as she evaluated the situation.

He brought the plane to a stop a short distance from the SUV.

Kaskae led the way to the plane and helped get the luggage out.

Atiqtalik greeted Alex and Trey and introduced Kaskae.

She thanked Clay who shook hands with both Alex and Trey. He added that he bet her a cup of coffee that he was right.

Alex nodded and said that she would add dinner to the bet and waved as he got back into the plane.

Northern Lights

Atiqtalik asked Alex what Clay was betting about and that she should be careful when betting with him because he seemed to always win his bets.

Alex shared the fact that he had a theory about the situation that she had been asked to look into and that losing to him would be a win for all of them.

As they walked up to the SUV Alex commented that the SUV had the same kind of tires that Clay had on his plane.

Kaskae laughed and said that the way his cousin drove the tough Bushwheels were needed. He said that his old pickup had regular tires because he could not drive so much better than Atiqtalik and he could not afford such expensive tires.

Atiqtalik shook her head, laughed, and said that she actually worked and had to drive thousands of miles over some really tough terrain and the tires were well worth what the forest service paid for them. She added that she was also a much better driver than Kaskae.

Alex listened to the two tease each other on the way to the cottage where they were to stay and knew that the two enjoyed the banter.

Ron Mueller

Northern Lights

Chapter 3: Out to the Pipeline

Atiqtalik again thanked Alex for her willingness to come out to help determine what had happened to her grand uncle. She smiled and said that she was taking both of them to a two-bedroom cabin that was used by visiting forest service members. She said that she had stocked it with some basic food goods so that they would not need to drive to one of the few places where a dinner could be ordered.

She admitted that it was also much less expensive for her to cover the costs. She had obtained permission from her superiors to use the cabin at no cost as long as when she was done' she made sure it was once again ready for use.

She asked whether that was acceptable to the two of them.

Alex said that it would make things easier and if it saved them time, she figured it was fine, especially since she knew that Trey was such a great cook.

Trey smiled, agreed, and added that he hoped that peanut butter and jelly was included in the supplies. And then he added that he hoped that Alex's snoring wouldn't keep him awake at night.

Atiqtalik laughed, commented that she was glad the two of them got along so well, then asked whether the two of them had come with some heavy-duty winter clothing.

Alex said that she had the heaviest winter clothing that she possessed and hoped that it would be adequate.

Kaskae added that if necessary, he could get additional clothing for her, but Trey was so much larger than most of the folks he knew but if necessary, they could make a trip to Prudhoe Bay where the store would carry goods for someone his size.

Trey commented that he thought he was well prepared but getting out for a day in the current weather would determine if the trip to Prudhoe Bay would be necessary.

The drive to the cabin took only a short time. The route went across some very open and sparsely covered areas then entered a more wooded location. The surrounding view was breath taking in its contrast to the parks Alex had been used to around Cincinnati where the various lush green full branched trees were many and large. The few pines in the valley seemed to stand in contrast to the mountains, the rocky terrain, and the vast expanse of sky. The rather large frozen snow-covered lake spoke very clearly to the cold that Atiqtalik had been talking about. It made Alex shiver just looking at it.

Northern Lights

Alex commented about the vast valley, stoney bare mountains and the contrast to the parks she had visited.

Atiqtalik nodded and replied that the snow had come early, there was more currently on the ground than she had been expecting this early in the season and she too knew how different the Gates of the Arctic National Park and Preserve was from all the parks in the lower forty-eight and even from the parks in the southern part of Alaska. She added that the desert based national parks were the opposites to the parks in the Arctic region.

A log cabin surrounded by pine trees with a thick layer of snow on the steeply pitched roof came into view. When they got ready to enter the log cabin, Atiqtalik shared the fact the cabin had been modernized and been remodeled. It operated on solar panels with a battery system that provided all the electrical power to run the lights, heated inside, and the water for showering. She added that showers needed to be short because the hot water heater was small.

The range used gas and its gas tank was the small portable kind since it needed to be inside because tanks outside would have to be heated.

The hood over the stove vented along a flat vent that ran across the wall and left the cabin as a cold exhaust. That vent only ran when the stove was being used.

She pointed to the end of the cabin that was a glass wall from floor to ceiling and said that it was a triple layer, air filled window that withstood the arctic cold very well. Then she pointed to two side coverings that she said should be closed at night or when the weather got really cold. It then would provide the same or better insulation as the rest of the cabinets. She added that during the winter the cabin was heated no matter if it stood empty.

She then suggested that they use the paper plates since washing the dishes would consume a lot of the water that could otherwise be used for the shower.

She then led the way to the bedrooms and said that each room had purposely been built in its own enclosure so that each was entirely inside the cabin with no wall to the outside. And each had insulation as effective as the outside walls. The rooms were effectively acting very similar to an igloo and a person's heat would heat the room to a comfortable level.

She pointed to the thick down filled looking bed cover and said that it provided all the warmth a person needed, though she personally found it a little too warm.

Trey commented that the cabin certainly seemed to be extremely well built and had been specifically designed to handle the northern cold.

Northern Lights

Kaskae said he had been impressed with the remodeling that the forest service had done. He added that he was trying to incorporate some of the things he had learned into his small home.

Atiqtalik suggested that they get situated and that in the morning she, Kaskae and her forest ranger partner would stop by around seven in the morning and they would go out to where Ignirtoq's snow scooter was located.

Once Atiqtalik and Kaskae had left, Alex suggested that they first call home since there was a four-hour difference in time zones and it would be getting late in Cincinnati. When she called, she found out that Matt was already out with his team, and Aurea was just getting ready for bed. She shared the details of where she was staying and then listened as Aurea shared what she had learned about the area.

Alex said good night and then called Matt and let him know she had arrived safely. The call did not last long because he was on a run on the way to the hospital.

After her calls, Alex looked over what was available to prepare for dinner. She found that the most interesting thing was a cut of caribou that looked very much like a thick T-bone steak, some yellow beets, and some potatoes. She checked with Trey about that combination and then began preparation of dinner.

Trey was online talking with Lesley until dinner was ready.

After dinner they both said that they needed to get some rest so that they would be ready to go looking for Ignirtoq in the morning.

Trey gave a laugh and said he would wash the dishes which was joke since it consisted of only the flatware and disposing of the paper plates.

Morning came much too quickly and once again Alex was in the kitchen area making a pot of coffee when Trey came in and said that he would fix breakfast and asked if two eggs some bacon and a couple of pieces of toast with jam would be sufficient.

After breakfast they heard a knock on the door and let Atiqtalik, Kaskae, and another ranger in.

Atiqtalik introduced her partner, John, and said that he was dropping off four snow scooters before he went out to check to make sure that everything in the park was as it should be.

She added that the four of them would be travelling to the pipeline on the snow scooters. She said that this would give Alex and Trey the opportunity to get some skill on them before they got to the pipeline.

As Trey and Alex got ready both she and Kaskae were checking on how the two of them were dressed for the cold. Both of them were congratulated on having on the right clothes and each of them were asked about the extra layer of a material that Atiqtalik was not familiar with.

Northern Lights

Alex explained that the extra layer was a bullet proof vest and pants that each of them were wearing.

Atiqtalik said that she hoped that there would be no gun fire.

Alex smiled and said that she hoped for the same thing but if someone had killed her great uncle, she and Trey were operating with the expectation that there was someone out there that was armed and dangerous.

Kaskae said that he did not own any bullet proof vests.

Atiqtalik said that her vest was with her partner since she had been focused on searching for her grand uncle and had not thought about someone shooting at them.

By the time they reached the pipeline, Alex and Trey were both enjoying their scooters and had tried a variety of maneuvers that both Atiqtalik and Kaskae had demonstrated.

Grayson was sitting in his hunting blind enjoying his coffee as he had done for the last several days. He had parked his camouflaged snow mobile behind the blind. He had walked out halfway to the river bend and verified that his setup was virtually invisible to the casual observer.

He had found the hidden snow scooter and had figured out how the person he had shot had gotten to the area. He figured that if he had not killed him then that person would return to get the scooter. He then planned to finish the job and then haul the body some place far away.

Ron Mueller

He first heard and then saw the four approaching snow
scooters. They headed directly to where the scooter was hidden
in the slight depression in the ground, so Grayson figured they
were associated with the person he had shot. In fact, one of them
was dressed very much like the person he had shot.

He picked up his rifle and looked through the scope. He
picked out the person that looked like they were associated with
local law enforcement and might be armed. He was just pulling
the trigger when one of the other persons in the group stepped
suddenly forward and knocked his target down as he pulled the
trigger.

At the same time as he felt the kick of his rifle, he felt the
bullet hit him in in the chest. He could not believe that anyone
with a handgun could have hit him and have done so with such a
lightening reaction. He put his finger where the bullet had
penetrated his thick jacket. His instinctive reaction had been to
fall backwards off of his chair. He knew the only reason he was
alive was because the jacket had been heavy enough to stop the
bullet that had no power left to penetrate all the way to his chest.
He was still in shock from having been hit as he turned and
crawled out to his two wheeled power scooter as two more
bullets hit the ground behind him. He was not sticking around to
duel with anyone that could shoot like he had just experienced.

Northern Lights

Alex saw the laser beam target Atiatalik's back. She stepped forward, gave her a push and at the same time felt a bullet hit her in the side. She instinctively fired in the direction of where she felt the shot had come from. She heard Trey's two shots as she jumped on her snow scooter and went zipping toward where she had shot. She heard a second scooter and knew that Trey was right behind her. She could finally make out the camouflaged blind and saw a scooter throwing up a plume of snow far out on the horizon. It was well out of firing range.

She stopped at the blind and examined it and the surrounding. It was clear to her that whoever had been using the blind had done so for several days and was prepared for whomever showed up to retrieve the hidden snow mobile.

Both Atiqtalik and Kaskae had followed Alex and Trey up to the blind. Atiqtalik asked how Alix had known to push her. When she learned about the laser beam, she asked if Alex had been hit.

Alex put a finger into the hole in her coat and said that her bullet proof vest had stopped the bullet, but she was going to have a nasty bruise since it had been some sort of high-powered rifle. She figured the bullet was still somewhere in her clothes.

She then knelt down and let out a deep breath along the handle of the chair and was rewarded by several fingerprints. She took out her phone and took close up pictures. She did the same with the cup that she picked carefully up and again was rewarded with several fingerprints that she took pictures of.

She sent the pictures immediately to Johnnie with a message for him to identify who they belonged to.

Atiqtalik said that she had never seen anyone get fingerprints in that manner.

Trey laughed and said that neither had he, but he was not surprised by anything his partner did. She had destroyed a coal barge and a helicopter gunship, and she had only had a fishing pole when she took on the gunship.

Kaskae shook his head and said that now he knew why his father had insisted that Alex should be the one to come and solve his murder case.

Alex said that they should see if she could lose her bet to Clay who had bet that his father was still alive. She said it was time to either find a dead body or to call Ignirtoq back to life.

She looked from the blind down to the bend in the river.

She asked how Kaskae would call to his father in his native language if he were alive.

He said that he would call out "Atelihai, Uana, naluanmiutun, and let his father know that the person who shot him was on the run.

Alex thanked him and said that she was betting on Clay being right and she was going to walk along the riverbank and call out to Ignirtoq and see if she could get him to show himself.

She said they should all follow her.

She left he scooter by the blind and walked to the bend and in a loud voice she called out, "Atelihai, Uana, naluanmiutun, Alex and I am calling you to come out and let us know that you are alive. The person who shot you is on the run, and we need your help to pursue him." She repeated it several times and then she stood looking up and down along the river and repeated what she was saying several more times.

Suddenly a voice behind them quietly said that he was quite eager to help.

Alex turned and smiled and shook his hand. She added that she had just lost a bet to Clay, and she was very glad that she had.

Kaskae gave his father a hug and said that he had been very worried about him.

Atiqtalik said that he had cost her a small fortune to get Alex and her partner to come to Alaska.

Ignirtoq said that he had the money, but he knew that the only way to get Alex to come was to die.

Alex nodded and said that he had been right and now that she too had been shot, it had become an actual case, and she would be pursuing the person who had shot her. She added that she hoped that his knowledge of the north would make her hunt successful.

Ignirtoq's eyes got large, and he asked how badly she was wounded.

Atiqtalik let him know that Alex had taken the bullet meant for her when she had stepped forward and pushed her out of the way.

Alex said that she was going to use all the hot water in cabin when she showered and afterwards, she was going to put on some salve that would reduce the pain and finally she was going to need to lay down.

Ignirtoq asked if she did yoga and smiled when she replied that she did.

He suggested that she lay down in her bed and do the Savasana pose and let herself relax and go to sleep.

Alex smiled, nodded, and said that she would do as he suggested.

She then asked where he had been hiding.

Ignirtoq walked over to the riverbank's edge and pointed into the small cave like enclosure. He smiled and added that he had the Savasana pose and had reduced his breathing rate and spent much of the time sleeping.

She then said that she was going to go back to the cottage and that she would see them all for breakfast in the morning.

Once she and Trey had returned to the cottage, she said that she was going to take a few minutes to talk with Johnnie, the Chief and to Matt. She commented that she had not anticipated an immediate gun battle, but she once again knew that she had spent her money well in buying the Kevlar outfits.

Trey asked if she was up for a BLT and a large glass of milk as a substitute for a larger meal.

Alex nodded and said that she would be ready for that after her shower.

Northern Lights

<u>Chapter 4: In Pursuit</u>

Grayson kept his snow mobile going full throttle as he sped away from the pipeline. He was still in shock that anyone could return fire so swiftly and accurately with only a handgun. He figured he needed to get out of the area as quickly as possible. He figured that he could get to Fairbanks by morning once there he would decide what to do next. He knew he needed to lay low. He wondered if he had left anything behind that might get him identified.

He counted on the fact the local rangers would not have any sophisticated way of figuring out who he was, but he had not been prepared to make a run for it. He decided that he should act like they knew who he was.

His best bet was to plan on a hunting vacation in Canada. He drove all night and made it to Valdez early in the morning. He called and arranged for a flight into Canada. Then packed his hunting duffel with all the equipment he needed, put his rifle in its carrying case, went to the bank and withdrew thirty thousand dollars and headed to the airport.

He would buy an all-terrain vehicle and get his hunting permit on arrival in Canada and then head for the woods. He was going to disappear for several weeks.

In Cincinnati, Johnnie was running the fingerprints that Alex had sent him. When he ran it against the Alaskan police data bases, he found that they belonged to a Grayson Gagnon who had a couple of speeding charges but otherwise did not have a record.

He sent the information to Alex.

Alex was pleased to get a quick hit on the prints. She called and talked with Johnnie and asked him to find out Grayson's address and all the information that he could find on him.

Ignirtoq arrived at the cottage for breakfast.

Alex shared what she had learned and said that she would soon know where his attacker lived and then she planned to go there and if he was still around, she would arrest him but if he was not there she would see if she could learn where he had gone and then pursue him.

Ignirtoq asked if he could accompany her and Trey.

Alex said that he could, but he could not participate in the capture.

They were still having breakfast when she got a call from Johnnie. He let her know that Grayson had a house in Valdez and gave her the address.

Alex asked if Ignirtoq knew how to contact Clay and arrange a flight to Valdez.

Northern Lights

Ignirtoq said that he could. He used Alex's phone and placed a call to Clay and arranged for a flight from Bettles to Valdez for three people. He agreed to a flight at ten and that he would bring everything to the end of the runway flight parking area.

Alex smiled and said that he was welcome to come along but when they got to Grayson's address he would need to stay with the car when she and Trey approached the house.

Ignirtoq nodded and said that he would follow her lead in the hunt for Grayson, but he wanted to be on hand when they finally captured him.

He said that he wanted to arrange for a modern phone when they got to Valdez.

When they met Clay at the airport, Alex smiled and said that losing the bet to him was one of the best things that could have happened. She added that if things worked out, she would take him to dinner that evening at the place of his choice.

He smiled and said that his favorite place was right on the harbor, and he was looking forward to splurging on her dime. He looked over at Ignirtoq and thanked him for staying alive.

The flight down was uneventful but finding a rental car was almost impossible. They ended up settling for an old pickup truck that one of the people at the airport rented to them for cash and their promise to bring it back by morning.

Trey drove the pickup and followed his phone's map to the address. He drove by and they were able to see a large pickup in the back with a snowmobile in it. Trey parked a block away and he and Alex got out of the pickup, took   off their heavy coats and put on a light jacket.

They then made their approach with their guns drawn and at the ready. Trey stood in the driveway where he could see both the front door and the pickup truck.

Alex approached the front door and called out that Grayson was under arrest and that he should come out with his hands up. She got no response. She knelt down to the side of the door and picked the lock and slowly opened and again shouted out her order. She then went in and slowly made her way through the house. It was empty.

She had Trey come in and help her with a quick search to see if there was anything that would give them a clue as to where Grayson might be going.

Trey found a series of hunting brochures that described hunting lodges in Canada. He also found a gun rack with several rifles and pistols in it. There was one empty rifle rack and one empty pistol holder.

Alex looked over the array of boxes of bullets and determined that the rifle that was missing was likely a 7 mm rifle.

She said it was time to get back to the airport to see if they could get more information about where in Canada Grayson had gone.

Northern Lights

When they got back to the Airport, Clay was still there talking with some of the other pilots. He said that he would check to see if any of them had made a flight into Canada.

Not long after he returned and said that a Grayson Gagnon had purchased a one-way ticket for himself. He had declared two weapons that cleared customs in Canada. He had a large duffle bag, in which he carried all of his hunting equipment and a separate smaller duffle with his clothes. The pilot said that it was clear to him that Grayson was a skilled hunter and carried only the essentials.

Alex decided that she needed to make a few calls to her Canadian Mounted Police friends and arrange for their help.

She first put in a call to the Chief, apologized for calling so late. She then brought him up to date on the case. She let him know that she was in pursuit of the person who had shot her and also the person who she had come up to find. That person was alive and helping her to pursue the shooter.

She went on to let him know that she was going to contact the head of the Canadian Mounted Police and asked him to do the same.

The Chief agreed to make the call the first thing in the morning. He told her to be careful but to bring this Grayson person in or to do whatever she had to.

Alex then called Johnnie and apologized to him for the late hour, but she needed to make sure that he locked Grayson out of his bank account.

Johnnie let her know that he had already done so, and he saw that thirty thousand dollars had been withdrawn the day before.

Alex thanked him and after hanging up she said that it was time to pay off her gambling debts.

Clay said that he could show her the way to the restaurant. He said that he would make sure they got one of the tables with a great view of the harbor.

While they waited for the order, Alex called and made hotel arrangements. She said that she hoped to be able to fly into Canada late the following afternoon. She explained that she hoped to get the support of the Royal Canadian Mounted Police.

Ignirtoq asked how she had such a close connection with the top brass in that organization.

Alex explained that she and her team had solved a case that had stumped them and had their support in several battles along the US–Canada border.

Clay said that he was getting more impressed each time he flew her somewhere. He asked if she needed a regular bush pilot.

Alex laughed and said that after her call in the middle of his night, her boss most likely would like to hire him to fly her somewhere in Canada and leave her in the bushes.

Alex went to bed early that evening because she wanted to make the calls to Montreal which meant that she would need to get up at three in the morning since she wanted to talk with Reginald Sailor, Reg to her, the head of the Royal Mounted Canadian Police when he came into the office at eight.

Northern Lights

She got through to him exactly when he came into the office. He was surprised to hear from her but said that it was a pleasant surprise and wondered what she might be calling about. When he heard what had happened and that she was wanting to get the support of the RCMP, he said that he would make a call to the regional leader and have his folks at her disposal.

He added that she should give the person she was pursuing a chance. He gave her the name of the regional commander but added that he doubted he would be greeting her personally since he was recovering from having his horse step on his foot.

Alex thanked him and said that she would be flying into Canada that morning and hoped to track down the person she was after and if she were lucky, she would have him in custody by the end of the day. She added that so far the person she was pursuing had been able to be just one step ahead of her.

The call had taken only a short time and Alex decided to get back under her blankets and see if she could get a couple hours of sleep.

She woke up a short time later and went down to the hotel's breakfast area. It turned out that breakfast could be ordered. After placing her order, she poured herself a cup of coffee and had taken the first sip when Trey came over to the table. Soon, Clay and Ignirtoq came over to the table.

Alex let them know about her call to the RCMP chief and the fact that they would be greeted by some of them when they landed in Chilliwack, Canada.

Ron Mueller

Clay said the flight would take several hours.

Grayson landed in Chilliwack, waited for his rifle to clear inspection, and then immediately looked for a snowmobile to buy. He wanted to get out into the forest and disappear. He found a used one that was the size that he wanted. He didn't bargain too hard because he wanted to buy it and disappear. He loaded his equipment on it and headed out into the forest.

He had purchased three hunting permits for deer, elk and for bear. He did not plan to use all three permits but he wanted to have a permit so he could shoot which ever animal crossed his path first.

A day later he shot a deer and quickly skinned, cut it up and disposed of what he did not want. He set up his camp about a mile from where he had downed the deer.

He had brought salt, pepper, some onions, garlic, and a cast iron frying pan with him. He prepared a boneless steak to fry, and he also cut some of the meat and skewered it and roasted it over the open fire. He sat enjoying his dinner.

He thought back over what he had just experienced. He was not sure who he might have engaged but he was sure who ever it was they were formidable enemies and he needed to lay low until they tired of looking for him.

He heard but did not see a helicopter but decided to douse his fire just in case it was putting up a plume.

Northern Lights

About the same time the helo was flying over where Grayson was camping, Clay was almost to Chilliwack. He taxied into the area where he was directed by the tower and commented that it seemed that a small army of red coated RCMP mounted on great looking horses were waiting to greet them. He brought his plane to a stop and turned off the engines.

Alex was the first to exit and was greeted by a young looking RCMP woman officer who introduced herself as staff sergeant Delia Tislen.

Alex shook hands with her and introduced Trey, Ignirtoq and Clay.

Delia said that she and her squad were to help in hunting down a fugitive that had entered into Canada to escape being caught. She said that she had a helicopter searching the area looking for any signs that might indicate where he might be hiding. She shook her head and said that there was a lot of forest to disappear into and she hoped that her folks could find out where that fugitive might be.

She then looked at the suitcases and suggested that they go to the lodging that she had arranged and get situated. She asked if the three of them could ride horses.

Alex nodded and said that she would love that and that she would work on relieving her muscles after each day of riding.

Delia smiled and said that she had long ago learned to relax and just blend with the motion of her mount. She said that matching the rhythm was the secret to not having a butt or back ache.

Ignirtoq grunted and said that his old body would be the one that would be complaining the loudest about bouncing up and down in the saddle, but he was determined to keep up.

Delia said that she had arranged for a large trailer to be set up at a nearby campground where they could stay. This would simplify the logistics of getting out into the forest. She and her team would be staying in the same campground as well but would be at the edge of the campground where they could also keep their mounts. She commented that the campground owners were pleased to have the business since things had been slow.

Once they arrived at the trailer and had all their belongings put in the trailer Delia suggested they make sure all of them got along with their horses and afterwards they could catch dinner at a local Bistro.

Alex made friends with her blond maned female mount that towered over her by introducing herself as she gave her an apple. She scratched it behind its ears and spoke to her quietly. She then mounted her from the left side and settled comfortable into the saddle.

Northern Lights

She watched as Trey expertly got on his mount that was at least a hand taller than her mount. She almost burst out laughing as she watched Ignirtoq being helped up into his saddle. He had trouble getting his foot into the stirrup and swinging his leg over the saddle. It was clear to her that he would be the one that would most likely be sore.

They went out for a short ride and then returned to the edge of the camp where the RCMP unit was camped.

Alex got off her mount and thanked her for the great ride and then began to loosen the saddle. She was relieved by a sergeant who took over and suggested that she go with his boss to have dinner and then get some shut eye.

The restaurant was just over a mile away and soon Alex had her order for an Elk steak in wine sauce in and was engaged in conversation with Delia. She learned that Delia and her team had all hastened to meet her and that the makeup of those that she had with her came from several locations in British Columbia. She was out of the British Columbia divisional headquarters located in Vancouver.

She and the rest had been waiting for most of the morning for her arrival at the request of Alex's RCMP friend and her bosses' boss. Delia asked how Alex had befriended the top Canadian RCMP leader.

Alex briefly explained the case that she termed "The Sins of the Daughter," to a wide-eyed Delia.

Delia commented the case had become a legend in the rank and file of the RCMP. She now understood the order to support and do whatever she was asked to do.

The dinner table went silent as they all dug into the food that had been brought out.

After dinner, Delia suggested that they take a car ride to see some of the scenic sights while they waited for any message that might indicate in which direction they should ride to investigate a potential sighting of a camp.

They spent a significant amount of time sightseeing and chatting as they waited for some sort of sighting that would give them a direction to go to investigate.

They had just returned and were getting ready for the evening when a call came in about the sighting of a plume of smoke. They got the coordinates and when they looked at the map Delia suggested they get an early start the next day and ride out to check on the person or persons that might be at that camp. She added that the chopper noticed that the plum they had seen disappeared almost immediately, so she figured that someone was trying to minimize the chances of being spotted,

After having doused his campfire, Grayson decided to move his camp south about a mile. He did not want to be surprised and figured that the move would ensure that he would continue to be left alone.

He went back along the trail that he had made and used a tree branch to eliminate the tracks his snowmobile had made.

Northern Lights

He gave up the camouflage activities after doing about a quarter of the distance. He walked back to his snow mobile and set up a new camp. He figured he would cook his dinner and make a stew in his frying pan and heat it when he made a morning coffee. He would then not light a fire until late the next day.

He figured that he would go out and hunt for rabbits and other small game. That would give him something to do during the day. If he tired of hunting, he figured he would read one of the books he had brought with him.

He felt confident that he had made his getaway and figured that he was in a land where he could remain invisible for as long as he needed to.

Ron Mueller

Northern Lights

Chapter 5: Plume Coordinate

The morning darkness had not yet given way to the slowly rising sun when Alex, Trey and Ignirtoq walked back to where the RCMP unit was camped.

Delia led them to the three horses they would ride.

Once again Alex first greeted her mount and spent a few moments giving her a half of an apple. She had given the other half for Trey to give to his mount. She then mounted and said that she was ready.

Delia asked if they had come prepared to spend the entire day out. She added that she had prepared some sandwiches and had water as well.

Alex nodded and said that she had made some sandwiches as well, but she was sure the three of them would welcome anything that Delia had to feed them.

The sun slowly crept across the forest and the tall brown barked pines seemed to have a mystical life of their own as they swayed gently in the light breeze. Alex seemed to breath in the scent of the pine and feel a magical power surrounding her. The rhythm of the slow trot of her mount was calming. She thought about what might be ahead. She opened her jacket to ensure she had easy access to her weapon. She took off her right glove and rode with her right hand in her pocket.

Trey was also riding easy and noticed Alex getting ready. He followed her lead, opened his jacket, and removed his right glove.

Delia was focused on her map and had her team zeroing in on the coordinates that the chopper pilot had given her.

When they arrived at the coordinates Delia thought at first that a mistake had been made because there seemed to be nothing there, but Ignirtoq got down from his mount and examined the area and then said that whoever had camped there had tried to erase their presence. He then said they should follow him.

He walked slowly along but said that the track was rather easy to follow. They had gone along slowly until the point where the tracks of snow mobile were no longer covered.

Delia had three of her team ride three abreast in front and her, Alex and Trey rode behind them.

Alex asked whether the three in front had bullet proof protection.

Delia said that all of her team had protection. She asked about Alex, Trey and Ignirtoq.

Ignirtoq spoke up and said that he did not have any protection.

Delia asked him to ride behind all of them.

Northern Lights

Alex said that she and Trey had their protection on.

They had just finished that discussion when suddenly one of the lead officers seem to fall off the back of his horse and then the sound of gunfire reached their ears.

Alex kicked her mount and galloped forward as she fired her weapon toward the small target that she could barely make out. She was trying to get close enough where her accuracy would greatly increase.

She felt more then saw Trey riding parallel to her and also firing his weapon.

Grayson was just enjoying his morning coffee when he took a moment to scan the area from which he had come. He was amazed to see what he took as a small army of red coats. He knew that the RCMP was coming his way. He aimed, shot the middle rider, and saw him fall off his mount. Then he immediately ripped down his tent and threw everything he had into the carrying basket in the front of the snow mobile. He had just gunned the throttle when he felt a sting across his neck. He was shocked to have been hit. Then he felt two hits in the middle of his back and knew that he had to get away before the two riders shooting at him got any closer. He began a zig-zag course through the trees in hopes not only to put distance between him and the shooters but also to put trees in the way and block any clear shots.

During his zig zagging, he lost the tent and the chair that went with it. He saw his cast iron pan fly out and hit a tree. He succeeded in slowly pulling away from the two charging horses. He stopped looking back. He knew he had to get out of Canada and get across the border and into the US. He was a US citizen, and he had his passport with him. To be totally legal he needed to have his weapons go through customs, but he had no plans to visit any of the official crossing points. He was going to cross over and keep going south until he ran out of snow.

Alex quickly realized that she and Trey were not going to catch up to Grayson. She stopped, dismounted, and began to walk her mount back the way they had ridden. She picked up the frying pan. A short time later Trey picked up the tent and chair. Neither of them were interested in the things for evidence.

They had all they needed to arrest Grayson what they needed was to capture him.

When they got back to where the camp had been, Alex spotted some blood in the snow. She knew that at least Grayson had been wounded.

She and Trey cleaned up the camp site and then proceeded to walk back toward where the RCMP group had gathered around the one that had been shot out of his saddle. He was still laying on the ground, but it was clear that he was not badly hurt because he was talking to Delia.

Ignirtoq asked if either of them had hit Grayson.

Northern Lights

Alex said that she had but evidently not bad enough for him stop.

She asked how far they were from the US border.

Delia looked on her map and said that it was about ten miles south.

Alex asked where there was an official border crossing point and found out it was back in Vancouver.

She thought for a moment and said that she needed to cross where Grayson had crossed and asked if Delia could make the crossing official and if she would lend her the three horses. They would return the horses once they had secured an alternate mode of transportation.

Delia made several calls and got clearance to act as the border inspection agent. She rode to the border with the three of them and wished them well and asked that Alex keep in touch with her and let her know how the pursuit turned out.

After getting across the border Grayson went about ten miles to the south and then headed west. He wanted to ditch his snow mobile and get a car or pickup so that he could drive off and not be found.

He rode the thick snow along the side of highway five forty-two and headed west.

He was looking for any vehicle that might be for sale.

Ron Mueller

He was going through Maple Falls where he spotted a car in front of the post office with a for sale sign. He inquired in the post office and found out that one of the postmen had the car up for sale. He bargained for it and was able to negotiate getting the car and using the snow mobile as part of the payment.

He put all his things into the car and headed out.

Alex had followed the snow mobile tracks and was coming along not far behind. She spotted the snow mobile parked in front of the post office and stopped and inquired about it and learned of the car sale.

The person who had sold the car said that for him it was a great deal because the snow mobile was worth more than the car and he had been able to get one thousand dollars on top of it all.

Alex got the description of the car and the license plate number and the direction that Grayson had taken.

Alex asked if he knew of any other vehicle that was for sale and said that he had seen a pickup with a for sale sign only a few blocks away. He looked at the three horses and asked what she was planning to do with them.

Alex said she was hoping to find someone to take them back to Vancouver and return them to the Royal Canadian Mounted Police.

He said that he had just the person she should talk to and for the right price she could get his buddy who had a horse trailer to take the horses back.

Northern Lights

Alex got that number and made the call and a few moments later a large six wheeled pickup pulling a four-stall horse trailer pulled into the post office parking lot.

The three of them watched as the horses were loaded.

Alex made the arrangements to get the horses back to Canada. She called Delia and got her in touch with the person bringing the horses back.

Ignirtoq shook his head, smiled, and commented that they had gotten the horses taken care of before they had their next ride.

Alex nodded and got directions to where the for-sale pickup was located. She led the way and the three of them walked to where the pickup was parked in front of a well-kept log home. She knocked on the door and was greeted by a young woman. When she asked about the truck, the woman called to someone inside that she called Sanders.

Sanders came to the door and Alex asked about the truck. He replied that he had bought it and then realized that it was a gas hog, and he could not afford to drive it the thirty miles each way to work. He said that it was a great pickup but just too expensive.

Alex asked him how much he wanted for it. He said that if she would take over the payments, he would be happy to let it go for what he had spent on it so far, which was five thousand dollars.

Alex agreed to the arrangement and asked for him to get online with her financial agent and arrange the money transfer.

She then called Johnnie and asked for him to make the transfer into Sander's bank account.

Trey had called the station, given them the description and the license plate number of the car that Grayson was driving and had a BOLO put out that described the driver as armed and dangerous. He asked that the location and direction should be noted but the car should not be stopped.

Ignirtoq asked the seller's wife if she could recommend a place where they could get a good meal.

She said that there were not too many places close by but there was a pizza place just a few miles to the west in Maple Falls.

Sander's shook hands all around and said that they had made his day, and he would be able to get a good night's sleep now that he had sold the truck.

Trey got into the driver's seat and turned the pickup on. He looked at the gas gauge and said that the first thing they needed to do was to stop at the gas station and fill up.

Ignitor said that after filling up they should go to a restaurant and get something to eat. He said that there were several restaurants just fifteen or twenty minutes to the west.

Alex contacted Bill and Trevor and asked them to monitor the response to the BOLO and asked them to contact her as soon as they figured out where Greyson might be headed.

They decided to stop for the night and get some rest.

Northern Lights

Bill called to let Alex and Trey know that the Washington State highway patrol was tracking Grayson's car. He had been spotted going down Interstate Five and then a short time later he had taken Interstate Ninety and that currently he was stopped in Cle Elum at a hotel.

The highway patrol was going to put on a tracking device that would allow them to track the car from the air.

Alex decided that the three of them should drive on until they were close to where Grayson had stopped so they would be in position if there was an opportunity to capture him.

Grayson was exhausted from escaping from Canada and then driving most of the day. He knew that he needed a few hours' sleep, and he knew that he needed to get back to the forest where he could once again find a place to keep out of sight long enough to have the search for him die down.

He got about four hours of sleep and decided he needed to drive on. Three hours later he was in Spokane where he decided that it was time to change cars.

He found a used car dealer and negotiated a trade for a pickup truck that had off road tires. He planned to cross into Idaho and go into the Idaho Panhandle National Forest where he would set up camp.

He drove on to Post Falls where he located a camping supply store and purchased the equipment he needed, additional ammunition and a deer hunting permit. He stopped a local grocery and bought some salt, pepper, onion, and some potatoes. He planned to hunt to get his meat supply.

At the border, the Washington highway patrol escort handed off to the Idaho Highway Patrol who greeted Alex back into the state. One of the officers joked that she had to stop chasing the bad guys into their state.

Sheriff Walter Wigger came online and said that he had learned of her chase and planned to join her.

Alex joked back with both of them about the fact that the bad guys must think that Idaho provided safe haven to them.

Once again, the day ended before Alex was ready.

She accepted a dinner invitation from Sheriff Wigers and decided to try and relax.

She made several calls back to Cincinnati and after spending time talking to both Aurea and Matt, she was ready for dinner.

Sheriff Wigger let her know that the highway patrol helicopter had spotted what they were sure was Grayson's campsite and they and his men would move in the following morning and make the arrest.

Alex thanked him and focused her attention on the menu and what she wanted for dinner.

Northern Lights

Grayson heard but did not see the helicopter, but its sound caused him to put everything into the back of his pickup and head out of the woods. He looked on his map and decided to head to Salt Lake City. He drove all night until he got to Pocatello where he got a room so that he could get a few hours of sleep before going on. His nightlong drive had given him time to think, and he had concluded that the hunt would only end when he killed his pursuers. He needed to devise some sort of trap where he could isolate the persons chasing him and then pick them off one at a time. He needed to find a place where he had the advantage of height and range.

Back in Cle Elum Alex got up for an early morning breakfast.

At breakfast Trey said that he wanted to purchase a rifle so that the next time they got a long range shot he would be able to respond. He said that he was looking to buy a 308 scoped rifle and a box of ammunition and asked if their budget would cover it.

Alex nodded and said that she was tired of shooting and hitting Grayson and not taking him down. She asked how much money he was talking about.

Trey shook his head and said he guessed somewhere between five hundred to a thousand dollars. He said that it depended on the exact model of rifle and the power of the scope.

Sheriff Wigger had come in at the tail of the conversation and said that he frequented a gun shop that had several 308s and a variety of scopes.

He would be pleased to take them there, but he suggested that they first go out to the coordinates that the chopper pilots had given them and that after the arrest buying the riffle might not be necessary.

Alex asked Trey if that sounded reasonable.

Trey nodded and said that he would wait and see. It they captured Grayson there would be no need for him to purchase the rifle.

Four highway patrol officers, Four of Sheriff Wigger's personnel and Alex and Trey left their vehicles about a mile from where the camp site was located. Ignirtoq followed behind them.

They spread out as they approached the campsite location and approached with their weapons at the ready.

Ignirtoq was keeping an eye on the truck tracks when he noticed a second set of tires that were leaving the area. He was wondering about them when they got to the campsite and found it empty. He said that he had followed tire tracks in, and he had spotted another set that might have been leaving but had not stopped to examine them.

He identified the spot where the pickup had parked and then he was able to identify the outward going tracks by the direction the tire treads pushed the dirt in the tracks.

This time he was in the lead as he followed the faint tracks back to the highway. When they reached it, they were about a half a mile from where all the squad cars had parked.

Northern Lights

Ignirtoq pointed down the highway in the direction where the pickup had gone. He looked at Trey and said that it was time for him to go to the gun shop because the next time they caught up with Grayson they might once again be dueling at long range.

Sheriff Wigger said he would take them there. He said that if Grayson continued to stay on the main highways the highway patrol would spot him, and they would know where they needed to go. He added that at the local speed limit and the eight-hour head start they had to figure that he was somewhere five hundred miles away.

Alex found it hard to stay put but decided to do so until they could get the next location where Grayson might be. She went to the gun shop with Trey and watched him pick out the 308-sniper rifle and scope. Trey also selected a hard carrying case that had space for the rifle, scope and one box of ammunition.

He asked where he could site it in, and the Sheriff took them to a local gun range where Trey spent a short time sighting in the rifle. He had Alex take a few shots and then put everything into the carrying case and said that he was ready for their next encounter with Grayson.

Ron Mueller

Northern Lights

<u>Chapter 6: High Ground</u>

It was almost noon when Grayson woke up. It took him a moment to get his bearings and to realize that he was in Pocatello in a hotel room. He was sure that his marathon drive had put him well away from his pursuers, but they had repeatedly been able to find him. He got up, showered, and then focused on where he planned to ambush the people pursuing him. He wanted a location that would ensure that he could see who was coming and where he would have a chance to eliminate all of those coming for him.

He was determined that whether it was one or a dozen he would be prepared to kill them all and he would have the tactical advantage that would let him.

After spending quite some time studying some detailed maps of the area, he found a small logging road that went out to one of the mountains to the east of the town. He decided to check that area out and see if he could find a location that gave him the advantage he was seeking.

He kept wondering how he had consistently been found. He had checked his truck, and all of his gear to make sure that somehow a tracking device had not been planted on it or on him.

Back in Cincinnati, Johnnie stayed online throughout the night and most of the morning tracking every cash transaction that had been made in a five-hundred-mile vicinity of where Alex was going. He skimmed over hundreds of cash transactions but none that were large enough or made sense in how it related to what Greyson might purchase. He was looking for a large gas purchase or a hotel stay and finally he found one at a hotel. He called Alex and gave her the name and address of the hotel.

Alex thanked Johnnie for providing her his magic touch and let him know that she was on the way there and that he should continue to see if he could get additional information on where Grayson might be.

Ignirtoq shook his head and said that he would hate to be the one running from her. He asked how this, "Johnnie" was able to figure out where Grayson had paid cash at a hotel.

Alex smiled and said that was the magic that Johnnie provided her with.

Ignirtoq asked if the magic was legal.

Alex said that she could not answer that without putting his life at risk for possessing such information.

He nodded and said that he understood and was glad that she had access to such magic.

Northern Lights

They spent the day driving to Pocatello and late in the day they checked out the hotel that Grayson had used.

Alex showed that desk clerks a photo of Grayson and verified that it indeed was him. She asked if they had any idea where he might have gone and learned that he had asked about a scenic peak that he would be able to drive to.

One of the clerks volunteered that he had shown him several logging roads that went out to two of the major peaks to the forest in the east. He pulled out a map of the area and pointed them out.

Alex looked at the time and said that they would be able to take a quick look at each of the locations to see if any of the roads had been recently used.

Ignirtoq asked the clerks when it had rained last in the area and learned that just two days previously it had rained uncharacteristically heavy. He thanked them for that information and said that he was ready to go and look at the roads that had been pointed out.

Alex took the time to make three room reservations before leading the way out to the pickup.

They checked out the four roads. They found what Ignirtoq said were fresh tire tracks on the third road. The fourth road had no fresh tracks.

The sun was setting as they returned to the hotel.

They spotted Elly's Diner and decided to give it a try.

Once they were seated Alex looked at the menu and said she was going to order the nine-ounce slow-roasted prime rib served with Yukon gold mashed potatoes with gravy, the seasonal vegetables and sweet onion rings with a cup of Illy's famous clam chowder.

Trey said he was going for the flat iron steak grilled with steak seasoning topped with steak butter and served with a baked potato with gravy. He added that he was also having seasonal vegetables and onion rings.

Ignirtoq gave his order for the beer-battered golden wild Alaskan cod, panko coated deep-fried shrimp that came with tartar cocktail sauce and lemon.

He then asked about what there was for desert and found out that the choice that evening was for a fresh lemon meringue pie with either a scoop of vanilla or pineapple sherbet. He nodded and said he would go with the vanilla scoop.

Alex and Trey both spoke up and said they would add desert to their order. Alex took a scoop of vanilla whereas Trey chose the pineapple.

During the meal, Trey said that he wanted to stop at the local hardware store and buy a half inch thick piece of plexiglass to put across the front window of their truck. He reminded Alex of how she had been saved from a sniper shot during their Sins of the Daughter case.

Northern Lights

Alex agreed that so far Grayson had been able to take a shot at them from a distance and had done so three times. He had shot Ignirtoq, then had shot her and the third time he had shot one of the RCMP riders that was in the lead. She figured that they should all want the plexiglass protection.

The next morning, they ended up going to three different shops before finding the plexiglass sheet that they were looking for. They ended up having to buy a full sheet and having it cut to the size that fit across the front window. They used the extra to have side window shields made. The plexiglass cost more than the rifle but Alex was determined to be able to take any long distant hit from Grayson and then get close enough to give Trey a chance at taking his shots.

She had the left-over piece cut so Trey could lay behind it and have some protection while he got his shots in.

She left the shop feeling that they were as well prepared as they could be.

They had breakfast and then went to the road that Ignirtoq had identified as the one that had the tire tracks indicating a pickup or a truck with similar tires.

Alex had chosen to drive. She had Ignirtoq holding the extra piece of plexiglass and Trey riding shotgun with his weapon pointed at the floor. She knew she was most likely sitting in the seat that would take fire.

Trey had chosen to buy a vest that had loops where he had put five cartridges. He wanted his hands free to handle his weapon and be able to quickly set up his firing position.

Alex looked over and said that he looked like a handsome movie star from one of the fugitive hunting movies.

Ignirtoq joined in and said that his sunglasses made him look more like a hired killer.

Trey looked at them and said that except that there were trees and grass, he felt like he was back in Iraq going into combat.

They had driven to the point where they could see a bend in the road and a cliff that had small pine trees and a variety of small bushes all trying to get a foot hold on the side the craggy stone face that towered high above them.

Alex slowed down to about ten miles an hour while she scoured the heights.

Ignirtoq commented that someone sitting on top would have a great tactical advantage.

Grayson was sitting on a stool watching for any incoming vehicle when a flash of sunlight exposed the incoming pickup.

He got down on the flat surface and set up his tripod holder and positioned his just purchased expensive 6.5 Creedmoor with a tactical strike scope.

He made himself comfortable, adjusted his scope and took aim at the driver of the pickup. He then slowly pulled the trigger and felt the confirming kick of the rifle on his shoulder pad.

Northern Lights

He saw the bullet hit the windshield and watched as the glass shattered into thousands of pieces. He was shocked that the pickup driver was still in control and driving.

Alex felt the hit in the plexiglass and the blast of air that blew in some of the windshield glass as most of it bounced off the plexiglass. She saw a series of boulders ahead and aimed the pickup in that direction. It exposed the driver's door window and suddenly it too exploded as a second bullet hit. She put the brakes on and skidded sidewards as she turned the steering wheel to the left.

She watched as Trey rolled out behind the boulder and was immediately joined by Ignirtoq who had carried the plex shield out with him.

Trey position the shield between the boulders and set himself up with three bullets on the ground out to his right. He then adjusted the tripod legs to the height he desired and then waited until he saw the glint of the scope at the top of the cliff.

A bush near the top of the cliff gave him the windage and he judged the distance and estimated the drop his 308 would take, then an instant later he smoothly pulled the trigger.

Grayson shot at the driver two more times. He was sure the disappearance of that individual meant he had scored.

Ron Mueller

He was taking a look for the other individuals when suddenly a burning pain went down his back. He crawled back from the cliff's edge and knew he needed to make his escape before he passed out from the burning pain. He turned and was dragging his rifle back to the pickup when he was hit in the leg by a second bullet. He felt the warm blood running down his leg. He got to the pickup and threw his rifle into the passenger's side, used his belt to make a tourniquet for his left leg. He got into the pickup and took off. The back window of the pickup shattered as did the butt of his rifle. He first reaction was to curse the fact that he had just lost the use of a great piece of hardware. His second reaction was to start worrying about the blood that he saw in the seat around him and the pain that was radiating from his back wound. He wondered who had the skill to make such shots.

He drove out through the forest until he knew he had to stop and treat himself as much as he could. He needed to get away and find a place where he could hide and recover.

Alex cautiously sat up behind the steering wheel and scanned the cliff with the binoculars that she had purchased. Everything looked clear. She called for Ignirtoq and Trey to get back into the pickup so they could drive to the top of the cliff and see what damage Trey had caused.

Trey said that he figured he had gotten some sort of hit because the firing had stopped. He was just not sure how much damage he might have done.

The drive up took them about fifteen minutes.

Northern Lights

Alex was disappointed to find that Grayson had once again escaped.

Ignirtoq got out and found the position from where the shooting had taken place. He pointed to the dark spots on the surface stones and loose dirt and said that Grayson had been hit at least once and had initially lost a lot of blood. He pointed to the spot where he said that Grayson had paused and to evidently stop the bleeding. He then walked over to where he said the pickup was parked and the turn marks made as Grayson drove his pickup away from the scene.

Ignirtoq followed the tracks to a point in the road and pointed out into the forest and said that the tracks headed due east down the mountain side. He said that he would follow the tracks through the forest. He added that he wanted to make sure they did not follow Grayson into some unseen ravine.

Alex saw a wide valley below ahead of them and Ignirtoq stopped and pointed eastward and said the tracks seemed to go out into the valley and probably into the forest ahead.

She shook her head and said that she was heading back to Pocatello, get new glass for the pickup and then get the highway patrol to locate Grayson once again or to find a hospital that had treated a gunshot wound. She asked Ignirtoq to get in and then she turned and drove back the way she had come.

Greyson stopped his pickup after crossing the wide valley. He looked behind him and saw no one following. He pulled down his pants and put some wadding into the bullet hole in the thigh of his leg to stop the bleeding. He took off his jacket and made sure the bleeding from the wound in his back had stopped.

He cleaned the blood from the front seat and decided to lay down in the back seat. He was able to lay on his stomach and get a brief rest.

Once back at the hotel, Alex contacted Johnnie and asked him to see if he could find where Grayson might be going.

She then called the Chief and updated him and let him know that Grayson had once again escaped but she was sure that Trey had wounded him so they were looking for where he might be treated for a gunshot wound.

Her final work-related call was to Bill asking him to renew the BOLO and alert the Wyoming and Utah highway patrol to be on the lookout for an armed and dangerous person.

She then called Matt and let him know that she was still in pursuit. She let him know that she planned to get up early and talk with Aurea before she went to school.

Matt let her know that he loved her and wanted her back in Cincinnati unharmed and in one piece.

She then asked Trey and Ignirtoq if they were interested in a Chinese dinner and asked the desk clerk if there was a Chinese restaurant nearby. It was close enough that Alex suggested walking.

Northern Lights

It was a cold but refreshing walk that helped relieve the stress that the afternoon had inflicted. They saw the restaurant when they were within a block and decided that they would order a variety of different menu items and then share.

After getting seated, Alex took on the role of placing the order. She looked down the menu and ordered an egg roll for each of them, an order of pot stickers, fried wonton, and salt and pepper calamari.

She then ordered mains of sweet and sour pork, sweet and sour shrimp, Beef with Sweet Pea Pods.

She asked Trey and Ignirtoq if they thought that was enough.

Ignirtoq smile and said that he was sure it was enough, but he also had his eye on the golden bread starter.

Trey laughed and said they should order the fortune cookies to see what their fortunes would look like.

After the order was in, Alex said that they were closing in on Grayson, but he was proving to be elusive and hard to capture. She said that now that he was wounded, they might be able to close in and finally make the arrest.

She added that they needed to go to get the windshield and driver's door window replaced before driving on.

She added that she hoped that by morning they would know where they were going.

In the morning Alex was surprised by a call from the front desk letting her know that her luggage had been delivered. It was a call that she had not expected and when she went to retrieve the luggage, she was surprised to see Clay standing with the luggage.

Clay said that he had been hired by Delia with instructions to get the luggage to Alex and to deliver a message that the horses were back in their stalls and had each been treated to an apple as a reward for their good service.

Alex gave him a hug and asked if he had time for breakfast before he headed back.

Clay said that he would love to have breakfast and that before he flew back, he was planning to sleep for most of the day because he planned to fly back to Fairbanks.

Trey and Ignirtoq came in and greeted Clay and thanked him for delivering their suitcases.

Alex led the way to the restaurant where they all ordered breakfast and chatted for a short time.

Trey broke the breakfast mood when he said it was time to find an auto glass replacement shop and ask for immediate service in replacing the windshield and side window.

Clay wished them luck in chasing Grayson down. He added that he was amazed that they had been able to track him down across a large part of Alaska, through Canada and now down four states in the lower forty-eight. He added that they needed to keep the state count down.

Northern Lights

Alex got the auto glass shop to expedite the work by letting them know that they were after a dangerous armed fugitive that had shot out the windows during a gun battle. She watched as four technicians all worked on the pickup.

The shop had a small store where they sold a variety of equipment. She bought a tarp to wrap the luggage in and a cooler to carry some drinks and sandwiches.

Once the glass was replaced, she had the plexiglass on the inside flipped so that the spot where the bullet had hit was on the passenger side. She then asked the shop to fasten the plexiglass to the windshield.

She gave the four workers a good tip and then the three of them returned to the hotel.

Now that she had clothes she planned to shower and change before driving on.

When they got back to the hotel, she placed an order for some ham and cheese and salami and provolone sandwiches with condiments in small packages on the side. She made the point that she did not want soggy sandwiches.

After taking a shower and checking out, the three of them looked on the map and decided to drive south to Ogden hoping to hear from someone about where Greyson might be.

Greyson had driven all night and was exhausted. He knew he needed medical attention. But if he stopped at a large hospital, he was likely to get arrested.

Ron Mueller

He looked on the map and saw the Uintah and Ouray
Reservation and figured that he could find a small local
emergency care facility where he could get the help he needed
and then escape somewhere to the east.

He drove past Ogden then caught interstate eighty-four and
then he took highway forty and drove into the Indian reservation.
He drove for several hours until he finally saw the sign for the
Uintah and Ouray treatment center. He hobbled in and let the
attending physician know that he had been accidently shot.

Once he was in the room with just the doctor and the nurse,
he took the nurse hostage and told the doctor to fix the wound on
his back first and then the wound in his leg.

He winced as the doctor worked on his back. He was told
that he was still alive because the bullet had lodged by his tail
bone. If it had exited, he would most likely have bled to death.

The doctor them looked at the wound in the thigh of his leg
and said that he was lucky there as well because no major arteries
had been hit. He then declared that he was done, and that
Grayson should let his nurse go.

Grayson said that he was taking her with him but that in thirty
minutes he would leave her unharmed at the side of the road as
long as there were no police chasing him.

He hobbled out to the pickup guiding the nurse at his side.
He got behind the wheel and when he looked at the gas gauge, he
realized that he needed to stop to fill up.

Northern Lights

He asked the nurse if she had a family and learned she had a seven-year-old daughter.

At the gas station as he was filling the tank he leaned in from the driver's side and told the nurse that he was going to let her stay at the gas station if she promised to wait thirty minutes before calling the police.

She promised that she would wait.

He looked at her and told her that if the police were to engage him before the thirty minutes he would return and shoot both she and the doctor.

He watched her shake her head up and down and swear that she would wait thirty minutes.

The nurse knew that she could wait thirty minutes and this crazed man would still be driving for hours across the reservation. She figured he was toast and would be captured before he left the reservation. She went into the station and bought herself a soft drink, took it out, and sat down in the chair that was just outside of the door.

Ron Mueller

Northern Lights

Chapter 7: Finally

Alex was looking out at the wide valley that held a few trees but was mostly yellowing grass with a few interspersed bushes. It seemed to stretch all the way to the horizon in both directions. There were a few traces of snow, but it was clear that winter had not yet hit in this region. Her phone rang and she knew that either Bill or Trevor was calling her.

Trevor came on and let her know that the BOLO had been answered and that Grayson had received treatment from a doctor at a facility on the Uintah and Ouray Reservation and headed east out of Bridgeland after filling his gas tank. He had taken a nurse hostage but had released her at the gas station unharmed and told her to wait thirty minutes before calling in any authorities.

Alex thanked him for getting the information to her after work hours and added that for her it was still daylight, and she was going to go to the care facility to see what she could learn and then she and Trey would decide whether to pursue or wait until morning.

Trevor wished her good luck and said that he, Bill, and Johnnie were trying to make sure she had the latest information and any help that she might need. He asked if there was anything else she might need at the moment.

Alex said that she needed good luck.

After getting off with Trevor, she put in a call to the highway patrol and got an escort to the reservation. They were greeted at the border of the reservation by a unit that took over from the highway patrol. They said that they had tracked the pickup that they were after until it had left the reservation. They said that they had wanted to stop it but had adhered to the instructions that came with the BOLO.

Alex thanked them and asked to be taken to the facility where her fleeing fugitive had received treatment.

Once they arrived, they were led to a meeting room where the doctor and nurse were sitting. Alex introduced herself and explained that the person who they had treated was fleeing from her because he had shot her, the person sitting next to her and a Royal Canadian Mounted Police. She pointed at Trey and said that he was the one that had wounded the person they had treated.

The doctor shook his head and said that each of the two wounds could have been fatal had they just hit slightly differently but as it turned out the wounds were significant but had not proved to be fatal.

Northern Lights

Trey nodded and said that he had tried his best, but the exchange of gunfire was at the maximum range of his weapon and except for the first shot the other three had been blind shots. He was surprised that he had hit his intended target twice.

As they were leaving the facility they got a call that let them know that Grayson was heading due south and had been spotted approaching Grand Junction and as far as the highway patrol could tell the pickup had not left the town.

Alex thanked them for the information and said that she was on the way.

Once they got to Grand Junction Alex wondered if Grayson was at some hotel or whether he had changed his mode of travel. She called Johnnie and asked him to see if he could figure out where Grayson happened to be.

It was an hour later that Johnnie called back and let her know that a one-way ticket to Fairbanks, Alaska had been purchased by a person calling himself G. Gay.

Alex thanked him went online and learned that it would take Grayson from fifteen to twenty hours to reach Fairbanks. She searched for a shorter flight and found one out of Denver that took only five hours. She called Alaska Airlines and was able to purchase three first class tickets.

She looked over at Trey and asked whether he could make the drive to Denver in two hours.

He smiled and said that she ought to arrange a highway patrol escort so that he would not get a speeding ticket.

Once they had their escort they made the journey about ten miles per hour over the speed limit. They had a lead and a tail escort that had their lights flashing and sirens wailing. It was a speedy journey.

Alex looked at Trey who was tapping his steering wheel to the rhythm of the flashing lights and humming the Marine hymn and knew that he was focused on getting to the Denver airport and to capturing Grayson.

Grayson was relieved not to be driving. He was exhausted. He figured that he could relax until he got back to Fairbanks. He could not believe that he had been hounded for the entire time he had left his house. He wished that he had never shot at that first nosy person because it had turned his life on its head. How he had been tracked still mystified him.

Alex thanked the men in the two highway patrol vehicles, she arranged for her pickup to be taken to the local impound lot where later she would have it handled. She then led the way into the airport.

She approached the first-class ticket counter and checked her luggage in and stood aside as Trey checked his luggage in. He then found out how to check his rifle in as well. He had to carry his weapon case to a special area to get it checked. The fact that he was a detective with the Cincinnati police helped expedite the process.

Northern Lights

Ignirtoq put his one suitcase on the scale and took his first-class ticket and followed Trey over to where the sniper rifle was being checked in.

They were escorted by a security person and taken through security. Then they were led by a gate agent to the plane. They had just sat down when the pilot greeted everyone and let them know that in five hours they would be in Fairbanks.

Alex sat back and thought through the chase that they had been on and marveled at the fact that they were now closing a loop that she hoped would end at the Fairbanks airport.

She called Bill and asked him to arrange to have the local authorities in Fairbanks meet with her so they could arrange Grayson's arrest.

Bill chuckled and said that she should just have stayed in Alaska and waited for Grayson to return.

Alex said that she agreed except for the fact that Trey had to shoot him to get him to return to Alaska. She heard Trevor say that he thought that both of them were dead shots and wondered how they could have missed Grayson so many times.

Alex smiled and replied that she still loved him in spite of his stinging comments.

Grayson was on his second lay over waiting to continue his flight to Fairbanks. He found a store in the airport that had some pain pills and took several of them in hopes that the pain in his back would lessen. He found it uncomfortable to sit so he decided to walk around while he waited to continue his flight.

He rued the day when he had taken that first shot and missed killing the person checking out his oil line tap. The irony was that he had no idea who that person was nor any of the other persons chasing him except for the Royal Canadian Mounted Police. All strangers to him and all determined to catch him. He hoped that the U-turn that he was taking would throw them off his trail and he could get back to the country that he knew.

The flight from Denver to Fairbanks was smooth and the service on the way there was as expected. Alex relaxed knowing that she would arrive well ahead of Grayson and would be able to arrange for backup from the airport security.

She was surprised when she and Trey stepped from the plane were greeted by an airport security guard that introduced himself and said that he was to take them to the lounge to get any refreshments they might want and then later he would return to have them meet with the folks who were prepared to help her make the arrest.

Alex asked who had contacted airport security.

He replied that he thought it was her boss, Trevor Carter, who explained the situation that he had assigned you to fly in and make the arrest.

Trey laughed and said that yes, the boss was always making sure that Alex was kept in line and doing what he had told her.

Northern Lights

Alex thanked the officer and said that she would enjoy the lounge until it was time to make the arrest. She asked that she have enough time to talk to all the folks to make sure the arrest was carried out with as little action as possible.

Once situated in the lounge she realized that there would be at least six hours of waiting. It was too late to call home, so she decided to take a walk around the airport and see what shops it had. She found one that had the Alaskan State flag on sale. She bought it for Aurea and added a bag of Ghirardelli chocolates to it.

Once back in the lounge, she asked Ignirtoq what he would be doing now that the chase was almost over.

Ignirtoq thought for a minute and then said that he was going to find every oil tap that had been installed and get them put on the drawings for the pipeline. He was then going to go fishing and try to get the thrill of the chase to die down so he could enjoy playing with his grand kids and have fun with all of his other relatives.

He asked her what she was planning to do.

Alex said that she was planning to enjoy spending time with her new daughter who she had recently adopted and hopefully get another invite to a grill out at Trey's home. She also planned on going on several long bike rides and get back into riding shape.

Trey said that he and his wife were trying to deal with having their only child away at college and having grill outs was one way that they dealt with that situation. He was sure to have a grill out in the next week or two.

Ignirtoq went back to the food line multiple times and commented that if he stayed much longer, he would need to join Alex on her bike rides.

The security officer came in and said that the team that would make the arrest was ready for her to talk to them. He guided them to an open area at the end of the passenger security clearance area where they were all standing.

She learned that the local police had sent a unit over to participate in the arrest and then transport that person to the detainment center until his arraignment.

Alex introduced herself, then introduced Trey and Ignirtoq. She gave a brief description of the long chase and of the various times they had exchanged gunfire with Grayson. She added that she wanted their support but that she and Trey would take the lead in making the arrest and only wanted them to get involved if Grayson put up some sort of resistance or was somehow armed.

She said that she was armed and would take any action that would be necessary, and they should keep their weapons in their holsters.

Northern Lights

Alex asked what gate the plane would use to deplane and then led the way there. She positioned everyone in a large circle around the exit area and instructed them to make their presence known but to keep back unless she called them into action.

The plane pulled up into position and the jetway was slowly positioned. Alex watched the first-class passengers as they came out. It seemed to her that everything was moving in slow motion. She knew that her adrenaline had kicked in.

She stood out in the middle area and watched the passengers walking out. She finally saw Grayson limping out of the jetway and raised her hand as a signal that she saw him.

Trey positioned himself to Alex's left and was ready to act if Grayson put up any resistance.

She walked up to Grayson and quietly told him that he was under arrest and that he should kneel down and raise his hands.

Grayson thought about running and took a step away from the person in front of him and then realized that there was a second person with her and then he noticed all the blue uniformed security guards and police standing ready in case he tried to make a run for it.

He raised his hands and said that he could not kneel down because he was wounded.

Trey pulled Grayson's arms behind him, put handcuffs on him as he recited the Miranda rights.

Once Grayson was handcuffed, Alex asked the police to take him to wherever the holding area happened to be.

Alex thanked everyone for providing back up. Once they were at curbside, she checked with the Fairbanks police who said they would take Grayson to the Fairbanks Correctional Center while he waited for his arraignment appearance.

Alex thanked them and said that she planned on returning to Cincinnati and hoped to attend the arraignment by video.

The officer in charge said that he had attended several arraignments where witnesses from some far parts of Alaska had participated in that manner. He was certain that she as the arresting officer could do the same.

She looked at Trey and asked if he knew what time it was and if they should plan to get a hotel and get a few hours' sleep.

Trey shook his head and said that he had no clue, but they should decide what to do after finding out when they could catch a flight to Cincinnati.

Ignirtoq let them know it was six in the evening. He said that he was calling Clay to see when he could get a flight to Prospect Creek and then decide whether to get a room.

Alex went to the ticket counter and found that there was a flight leaving for Cincinnati at ten that evening and arriving in Cincinnati at ten in the morning the following day. She let out a groan, looked at Trey who mouthed "let's do it."

They purchased two seats in first class, checked their luggage and then went to the lounge to wait for the flight.

Trey told Ignirtoq that he wanted him to have 308-sniper rifle and scope.

Northern Lights

Ignirtoq said he couldn't accept such an expensive gift.

Trey said then he would sell it to him for a dollar.

Ignirtoq took out his wallet and extracted one dollar. He said that he understood the concept and he was very pleased to be able to buy a great hunting rifle. He took the case and said that he would take pictures of anything he shot with it.

Ignirtoq said that Clay would be meeting him in less than an hour. He wished them a safe journey and said that his time with them was memorable in many ways but that it had been an honor to have helped in the capture of Grayson.

Alex gave him a hug and told him that he had been a great help and that she would mention that in her report.

When the plane finally departed, and Alex was situated she was able to sleep for most of the flight to Cincinnati. Once in Cincinnati and she got to the escalator leading to luggage claim she looked up to see Trevor waving to her.

He and Bill gave her a hug and complemented her on catching the bad guy and not killing him.

Alex smiled and said that Trey had provided the initial pain that Grason needed and now she hoped that the prosecutor and judge would put him away for the rest of his life.

Bill said that they had orders to make sure she did not come into work. He shook Trey's hand and complemented him on his shooting and told him that he was to go home as well. He added that Travis was driving Alex's old car and would take him there.

Ron Mueller

Alex arrived home close to noon and decided that she would take it easy but that she was going to bake a large batch of cookies that she could give to Johnnie and the rest of the team.

She put the Alaskan Flag and the chocolate on the kitchen table and then prepared the cookie dough.

She had just placed two warm cookies and a glass of milk on the table when Aurea and Mary came in the back door.

Aurea rushed over to her and gave her a hug and said she knew that she would be home. She had done her homework at school so she would be able to go out riding.

Alex gave Mary a hug and thanked her for watching Aurea while she was gone.

Mary replied that it gave her something to do during the day and she loved doing it.

Matt called and said that he would be home for dinner and asked if he should bring home their favorite Korean mix of starters and main menu items.

Alex told him to bring home whatever came to him and that she and Aurea were going out for a bike ride and would be back for dinner.

<u>Chapter 8: One More Time</u>

The next morning Alex followed Johnnie down the hill as they rode their bikes into work. They chatted over their headsets about the chase that Grayson had taken her and Trey on. Alex commented that it had been one of the more extended ones that she had experienced, and she was glad that it was over. They arrived at the station, and both took their bikes into the locker room and got into their daily work outfits.

Alex walked in with a cup of coffee and was pleased to see that Bill and Trevor were already there and had left the donut box on her desk. She took out a bear claw, cut it in half, and put one half on Trey's desk. A moment later he walked in and said that he felt like warmed over toast and hoped the bear claw and some coffee would put some energy back into his body.

The Chief walked in and came over and helped himself to a jelly roll. He congratulated all of them for having once again having worked together to solve their case.

Trevor nodded and said that "yes some of us had to do the grunt work and some of us got to do the exotic travel from Alaska through Canada and down the Rocky Mountains until they tired of the beauty and relaxation of it all and finally made an arrest. An arrest that did not have any gunfire associated with it," and in spite of that Bill and I still brought in donuts.

Alex laughed and said that the next time they should trade places and when he and Bill got back, she would buy the donuts.

Bill shook his head and said that he would rather not.

The Chief shook his head and said that he had real work to do and walked away toward his office.

Alex looked over at Trey and said that they should go to a huddle room and see if they could knock out the case report before lunch.

She and Trey were almost done with the report when her phone went off. It was the sound of a bear roaring and was the ring that she had assigned to Ignirtoq. She looked at the time and realized that it was only three in the morning in Alaska. She put the phone on speaker mode and said hello and asked why he was calling at three in the morning.

Ignirtoq said that he had just been notified by the police that Grayson had escaped. He added that he was going to be going on the hunt with a beautiful new 308-sniper rifle and scope that he had bought for a pittance from someone at the airport that had lost his mind and sold it to him for a dollar.

Northern Lights

He went on to say that he was sure that she would soon learn of the escape and that she should wait until he had his chance to hunt Grayson down before she did anything.

He added that he and Clay had gone out to celebrate and they had not left Fairbanks so there was no way Grayson knew where he was. He on the other hand was pretty sure that Grayson would go to his house in Valdez and get whatever he needed to once again hide out.

Ignirtoq chuckled and said that Grayson was on his territory and would find it hard to hide. In the morning, he and Clay would fly to Valdez, and he would see if Grayson had made it to his house.

He ended the call by thanking the two of them for having given him lessons on how to hunt Grayson down.

Grayson found it absurdly easy to break out of the holding cell. He had found a hairpin and had decided to try his luck at picking the door lock. He had positioned himself so that the camera could not see what he was trying to do. He played with the lock for less than ten minutes when suddenly he heard it click and the cell door was open. He saw that the camera in the hallway seemed to move to scan different parts and then repeat the cycle. He timed it so he walked away from his cell after the camera had scanned it. He walked slowly and steadily out of the holding area, out into the street and turned at the first corner. It was early in the morning and the streets were bare. He knew that he needed to get out of Fairbanks as quickly as possible.

Ron Mueller

He figured his best chance was to get to Valdez and to his house so that he could restock with what he needed to hide out. He looked ahead and saw a maintenance truck parked outside and all-night café. It had its engine running to keep its engine from freezing. He looked in the café and saw two men sitting at a table having a cup of coffee and chatting. He looked in the truck and was pleased to see a jacket and a brown Russian Ushanka hat. He walked around to the driver's side and put the truck into gear and eased it out into the street and drove slowly away. Once he had gone past the café, he turned on the head lights and headed for the highway that would take him to Valdez. He drove at the speed limit but was worried about having the police after the stolen truck. He drove until he reached station twelve of the Alaskan pipeline and pulled into the parking lot and parked at the far corner of the parking lot. He was on familiar ground and knew that all the vehicles would remain running, and most would remain unlocked. It was just past the starting hour so he would have an entire shift's time. He walked out through the parking area and noticed that there were several black pickups that all looked the same. He picked the one that was parked next to a tall white van that obstructed the security camera, got in and slowly drove out of the lot.

Northern Lights

At the gate he flashed his driver's license and drove slowly out. He smiled and waved at the gate guard and got on the highway. An hour and a half later he arrived in Valdez and stopped at Safeway, went in purchased a loaf of bread, mayo, a head of lettuce, tomatoes, a T-bone steak, a dozen eggs, fresh sausage, ground coffee and a quart of milk.

He drove slowly by the police station and finally arrived at his house. He pulled into the driveway and put the pickup in the garage. He took his groceries in and prepared himself a couple of fried eggs, several patties of sausage and buttered toast with strawberry jam. The fresh cup of coffee with cream and sugar rounded out the breakfast and made him feel like a freeman again.

He wished he could spend the night, but he figured that he needed to get the things that he needed and head out before the police came to check on what he was doing. He went to the box where he had stashed emergency cash and counted out what he had. He was down to his last fifteen thousand dollars.

He walked down to the house that had a car sitting out in the driveway with a for-sale sign and an asking price of three thousand dollars. After some bargaining, he got it for twenty-five hundred dollars and was able to keep the current license plates with the promise that he would get it changed that day.

He drove the car to his house, loaded everything that he thought he needed. This time he took most of his guns. His favorite of the lot was his Ruger American black bolt action that fired 7mm Remington Magnum bullets. He considered it the second-best rifle that he had owned and was sad that his favorite had been destroyed during the chase. That 308 had a greater range and more striking power but the 7mm had great accuracy and he figured that it would be his primary weapon as he once again headed out to disappear in the woods.

It never crossed his mind that in the lower forty-eight most people trying to hide headed into a big city to disappear whereas his desire to hide in the woods was a very Alaskan mentality.

Ignirtoq knew that he and Clay were at a slight disadvantage as compared to Alex because he did not have the resources to find where Grayson might have gone. However, he felt confident that one of the places he would go would be to his house in Valdez.

Clay flew into the airport and parked his plane. The two of them asked around to see if they could rent someone's car or pickup. One of Clay's acquaintances offered to lend him his pickup since he would be gone for a flight up to Prudhoe Bay. He asked that it be parked back where they got it.

Northern Lights

Ignirtoq said that he was pleased to have the use of the pickup, but he wanted to pay the going rate for its use. He walked out to the dark blue, large pickup with a full back seat and full bed. It was a huge pickup. He asked Clay whether he was comfortable driving it.

Clay said that it put his pickup to shame, and he was going to enjoy driving this one. He drove it back to where he had his plane parked and they got the things that they wanted from the plane. He took his long rifle twenty-two that used a heavily loaded cartridge that gave it extra distance and put it on the floor behind the driver's seat.

Ignirtoq took out his rifle case and put it on the back seat. He said that he didn't think he needed it while they were in Valdez, but he wanted it close at hand just in case.

They drove to the home address that Alex had given him but parked a block down the street and Ignirtoq took out his 308 and Clay carried his twenty-two. The two of them walked back to the house. They knocked on the front door and got no answer. The two of them walked around the side of the house to the garage. They looked in through windows and saw a large black pickup. They tried the back door of the house but got no response.

Ignirtoq commented that they were a little late getting there and Grayson had already left. They were driving out when he noticed a car for sale sign laying on the curb of a house and decided to stop and ask about it.

The young woman that came to the door said that they had just missed buying a great low milage tan Ford sedan that her husband had let go for a great price just that morning.

Ignirtoq asked if the car had a license plate and was able to get the license plate number. He thanked the young woman and then drove to the local police station.

Once there he explained the situation and after the officer there had called the Fairbanks Police the Valdez police went out the Grayson's house.

Ignirtoq accompanied them and was able to get an idea of what Grayson was up to. He found the bread wrapper and other things in the kitchen that let him know that he had stocked up on food and was planning to go out into the woods. He decided to stop at the local outfitter to see if Grayson had also purchased camping gear.

Once he found out the equipment that had been purchased, he knew that Grayson planned to go deep in the woods somewhere but he would need to be able to go in and out over time so he would need to be near some useable road. He studied the area map and zeroed in the area around the Glacier Lookout area. It provided road access and was out of the way. This would allow him to drive there and then hike into woods and set up camp.

He asked if Clay still wanted to accompany him.

Northern Lights

Clay said that it beat the mindless hours of flying that he often did. However, he wanted to have a good breakfast, a solid lunch and a good night's sleep before heading out into the woods. He said that he needed to stop one more time at his plane and get his winter gear so that he wouldn't freeze to death in the woods.

Ignirtoq admitted that he too needed to get the right gear to go into the woods after Grayson.

They stopped at the City Diner to have breakfast. They agreed to get a carry out lunch and that they would stop at the grocery and buy the goods to have what they would need for a couple of days. They then drove to where Clay had parked his plane and got the other things they needed.

The drive out to Glacier Lookout took them about an hour. The distance was only about fifteen miles but for half the distance they were on a single lane snow covered road. It had been cleared but it had snowed, and the going was slow.

Ignirtoq had called ahead and arranged to get keys for two rooms at the Valdez Glacier Campground where they paid for the rooms and got instructions on how to use the room heaters.

Just before they arrived at lookout facility they spotted where a car had been driven into the woods. They did not stop but they were now sure that they had made the right choice.

Ron Mueller

Ignirtoq said that in the morning they would walk back and then go from tree to tree as he tracked Grayson to his campsite. He pointed out that they would need to be very careful because Grayson had been able to get in the first shots each time he had been confronted.

The next morning, they both had a hearty breakfast of pancakes, eggs, and ham. They then made themselves sandwiches and filled a large thermos with coffee.

Clay joked that they were carrying more food than anything else.

Ignirtoq nodded and said that he hoped that they would capture Grayson early in the day, but he did not want to get exhausted, cold, and hungry because they had not planned ahead.

When they got back to where the car was parked, they verified that the license plate number was in fact the one that was on the car he had purchased. Ignirtoq began a slow and cautious tracking of where Grayson had gone.

He moved along the trail that had been lightly covered by snow but was very clear to him. He kept looking ahead through his scope trying to make out where Grayson's camp might be. It was close to noon when he saw a wisp of smoke. He said that they should stop and get a bite to eat because they should take off their backpacks and get ready for action.

After lunch he moved from tree to tree and each time he looked ahead to where he had seen the wisp of smoke. Finally, Ignirtoq was able to make out the camp.

Northern Lights

Grayson had selected relatively a place to get out of sight because he did not want to be caught out on the road. He had come up into the mountains as far as possible. He did not have the best car to negotiate the snowy roads or to think about going off road through the forest. He had done the best he could and driven up to one of the few very remote areas, driven the car off the single lane road and then covered it with snow so that it could not be spotted from up above. He then used a sled to pull all of his gear several miles into the forest. This time he had returned and spent time covering his tracks as best he could. He hoped that his path would be invisible from the sky.

He had brought a handful of books and planned to sit in his small tent where he could stay warm, read and to periodically make sure there was no one about.

Ignirtoq positioned his rifle across the fallen tree branch and took aim. He remembered Trey's instruction about the three-foot drop of the bullet at maximum range and about the effect of the wind. He took his first shot and saw a hole appear to the left of where Grayson was sitting. He quickly loaded the second cartridge, made he windage adjustment and fired again. This time he saw Grayson fall back into the tent.

Grayson was still trying to comprehend the action of the first bullet when he was hit in the chest and knocked from his chair.

Ignirtoq rushed forward to where he saw another fallen tree and got down behind it.

Clay was hiding behind a large boulder. He did not think that he could hit anything because he was so far from the camp, but he figured he might provide some misdirection, so he fired his weapon.

Grayson lay back for a moment and thanked the stars for having thought about buying a bullet proof vest. He recovered and crawled out of his tent and looked through his scope and saw the gunfire from behind the boulder. He estimated that the boulder was about four hundred feet away. He lined up his sights so that the next time that shooter exposed himself he would take him out.

Ignirtoq carefully sited in on where Grayson was laying behind the fire ring that he had made. He had his head, and his arms exposed. He knew that at this closer range the drop would only be about a foot. He did not want to get into a duel. He carefully took aim and was about to pull the trigger when Grayson rolled away from the fire ring and out into the open and fired his way.

The bullet hit a foot to his right, but he knew the next on would most likely hit him.

He was surprised when a bullet hit one of the fire ring stones and caused Grayson to once again roll away.

Clay waved to him from behind a tree that was at least ten yards closer than he was.

He ran forward and had just gotten behind a large pine when a bullet hit the tree.

Northern Lights

The gun battle that he had hoped to avoid was happening. He thought about how to best handle the situation and could not think what that might be. He thought about everything that Trey had shared with him and remembered Trey saying that sometimes the most effective way was to expose oneself and take a hip shot and then laydown and quickly take the kill shot.

Ignirtoq shook his head and felt that he was about to die but it might be a quick way to end the duel. He jumped out and gave a loud yell and took his hip shot as he fell forward. He ejected and loaded in rapid succession. He felt the bullet when it grazed his shoulder, but his sight zeroed in and he took his shot.

Grayson had figured out that he had two people shooting at him but the one that seemed to have the superior fire power was the one he needed to focus on. He was surprised when that shooter jumped out into the open, fired from the hip and fell forwards into the show. It threw off his first reply shot. He had his bead on the shooter when suddenly the world went black.

Clay hesitated a moment, but he realized that Grayson was either dead or wounded so badly that he was lying face down in the snow. He rushed to where Ignirtoq was laying and turned him over. He was hit in his left shoulder but smiled and said that he had learned from a war hero on how to take out the enemy.

He said that they should verify that Grayson was dead and then call the Forest Service to get their help.

Ron Mueller

<u>Chapter 9: Alaskan Hero</u>

Alex had been worried about Ignirtoq going after Grayson and had put out her feelers as to what was happening in Alaska. She got hold of Atiqtalik and Kaskae and asked them what they knew and then was more worried when both of them said that they had not heard anything. She called the head of the Fairbanks police and learned that Ignirtoq had gone to Grayson's house in Valdez and had found the stolen vehicle in the garage and had also identified an automobile that Grayson had purchased in his neighborhood.

She learned that Ignirtoq had engaged the Valdez police department and then had gone after Grayson based on where he might have gone. Alex doubted it was a random guess and figured that Ignirtoq had a good idea of where to look. She was relieved that Clay seemed to be going along. Clay, she felt would be the help that might make a difference.

She went into Friday worried about what was happening in Alaska.

Late Friday, Johnnie got a call that he knew would be a big relief to Alex. He agreed to work with Ignirtoq to make a video of the scenes of the chase and of the final confrontation. He said that he would need to let Alex know that the chase was over and that he was safe, but he would keep the rest as a surprise.

Ignirtoq said that he would call Alex and let her know how things had ended but he wanted the video to be a surprise.

Alex was indeed relieved when she heard Ignirtoq relate how he and Clay had worked together and had bested Grayson. He did not say more because he wanted to leave the details of the story to be part of the narrative for the video he was working on with Johnnie.

Alex focused her effort on closing the case. She asked Johnnie to move the money that Grayson had in his bank or invested, to a trust that would be used for the indigenous people in Alaska. She let Aurea know about the fund and asked her if she wanted to give it a name. Aurea thought about it and said that it should be called the Alaskan Black Gold Fund for Indigenous People, (ABGFIP). Alex let her know that she was going to be named as one of the executors of the fund along with Ignirtoq. Aurea asked what she would be doing as an executor. When she found out she said that would be a great project that she could write about. She added that she was going to study and write about the Inuit people.

Northern Lights

Alex went into the weekend with mixed feelings. She and Trey had done their best to put Grayson behind bars but by escaping he had taken the situation to another level. He had been prepared to resist capture for a second time. This time his pursuers knew how to prepare for the encounter and had been able to track him down almost immediately.

It made her sad that someone could live a life so apart from the society they existed in. Grayson had done nothing for other people or the community that he lived in. She wanted Aurea to be exposed to helping others and enriching the society around her.

The weekend caused her to focus on Aurea, Matt, and herself. On Saturday she led them on a long bike ride along the Loveland trail. She ordered a lunch for the three of them from one of the small restaurants situated along the trail. They stopped and spent time enjoying a slow leisurely lunch of chicken, mashed potatoes, green beans, and a small mixed vegetable salad on the side.

She then led the way up the trail until she recognized the shop that served a variety of ice cream. They stopped there and each had two scoops of the ice cream of their choice.

The ride back to their house took the rest of the afternoon. Once back at the house the next important event was to select a restaurant that they all agreed on for dinner. Once that happened Aurea got to select the food that was to be delivered. Alex smiled and said that Aurea could order anything she wanted as long as she also ordered some onion rings.

After dinner, Alex spent an hour jogging on the treadmill before saying that she was turning in early so she could get a few extra hours of sleep.

The next day they arrived at Trey's house early and she took a seat on the porch and accepted a lemonade and a tray of vegetables with a Thousand Island with garlic dip.

She enjoyed the snack and watching Aurea playing chess with Matt. As she watched she realized that Aurea was a better player than she was and that she was challenging Matt. She was happy when Sarah the neighbor girl showed up and the two of them went off to play together in the basement.

She was surprised when Lesley asked her to come with her to her bedroom where she wanted to show her the new dress that Trey had picked out and see what she thought of it. The two of them walked up stairs and Lesley commented that Trey had let her know that during the fugitive chase he felt like he was back in combat, but it was different because he did not feel the stress that he had felt then.

Alex wasn't sure what was going on, but she knew that Lesley was acting a little out of character. It was when they came back on the porch and Alex saw the rest of the team sitting in front of a large TV screen that she realized that Lesley had taken her to the bedroom to get her out of the way.

Northern Lights

Aurea was beaming and cried out that it was a surprise and that everyone in the family and all her close friends were online and ready to hear about the manhunt that she, Trey and Ignirtoq had been on and that Ignirtoq would be narrating a movie put together by he and Johnnie. She highlighted the Hawaii connection. Then the Chicago connection, the connection from Texas, the Alaska connection, and the Royal Canadian Mounted Police connection from Vancouver.

Everyone called out surprise in unison and then Ignirtoq came on, introduced himself and then he introduced the two main stars, Alex Evercrest and Trey McGregor. He showed the picture of his grandniece, Atiqtalik and his son Kaskae the two people he had to fool so they would pull in the greatest detective that lived in Cincinnati. He said that he had done this after he had been shot by Grayson Gagnon. He convinced his brother to call Atiqtalik and tell her that he had been fatally wounded and needed the best detective in the world to find out who had killed him. Atiqtalik had talked to Kaskae who was convinced that they were being conned by his father but if his father was determined to get this "Alex" person up to Alaska they might as well go along with him. The scene on the screen panned out on the bend of the river and took in the eight-foot diameter Alaska Oil pipeline. It then walked slowly up to where a snow bike was hidden under some brush.

He then had a picture of Alex looking at the camera and a picture of someone being kicked out of the way, Alex being hit by a bullet and then firing her weapon as she staggered backwards.

Alex chuckled and asked who her body double happened to be because the response shot was very slow.

Ignirtoq laughed and said that he had so many volunteers to appear in this movie that he was not sure who had played her role and he apologized for not having anyone that was tall enough to fill in for Trey.

Audre shook her head and commented her mother had not told her about getting hit by a bullet.

He then showed the tent that had been knocked down when Grayson had hurriedly left on his snow mobile, and it showed Alex running after him firing her weapon.

The next scenes were of Clay's piper cub getting loaded with their luggage and all of them getting on. Then the landing in Canada and being greeted by Sergeant Major Delia Zennesky of the Royal Canadian Mounted Police. The video continued as they were taken to the trailer where they spent only one night before they rode out on horseback to hunt Grayson down.

The shot that took down one of the lead RCMP was the first time that Alex had seen it, and she was surprised by the fact that the lead rider had survived without any major wound. The next scene showed she and Trey urging their mounts in the chase after Grayson.

Northern Lights

She laughed at both of their despondent faces when they rode back to the RCMP group.

It was also clear to her that Ignirtoq had improved on taking pictures because as they rode into the US, he was taking side shots as well as periodically getting some frontal shots. He got great shots of the pickup, interior. Shots of her and Trey and always the panoramic view of the country they were driving through. She wondered if Ignirtoq had a video early on during the chase.

Then the scenes were of getting the plexiglass shield put in and a few moments later it showed the shattering of the front and side windows. The video sound that was captured when the windshield seemed to explode seemed to amplify the scene. The next shots showed Trey preparing to take his four shots and the sound of and the smooth action of each of the shots. Then for a long moment there was silence and then her voice calling for them to get in the pickup so they could go to the top of the mountain to see how Trey had done.

The scene then panned on an empty campsite.

Ignirtoq had kept his camera running and a narrative of what he was seeing. It was the first time that Alex had heard it. She listened as he then gave a lesson on how to track the vehicle through the rough terrain. She looked around the porch, saw that everyone was glued to what was being shown and knew that everyone was enjoying the presentation.

The final scene was her and Trey arresting and having Grayson led away.

Then in bold letters the video displayed, "AND THEN HE GOT AWAY." "Time to refill your drinks and get popcorn."

The screen went black, but Ignirtoq's voice announced that he and Clay decided that they should see if they could end it all and prevent a replay of the first half of the video.

The video then began with Clay bargaining to use a friend's pickup that was outfitted for off-road hunting and going through the forest. Their drive to Grayson's home and their knocking on the front door, looking through the windows of the garage and seeing the stolen pickup and then approaching the back door and again getting no response. Clay could be heard asking how Grayson had left when the pickup was still in the garage.

The video continued and showed the car for sale sign as they drove out of the neighborhood. The conversation with the young housewife verified that Grayson had purchased a tan sedan that had been for sale.

Ignirtoq could be heard saying that Grayson would need to get some new camping gear because he had lost three sets during the chase. The next scene was in the camping outfitters and a discussion of the most nearby remote places to get deep in the forest. The old clerk took out a map and point out three different areas that he considered remote and hard to get into where the forest provided great cover.

Northern Lights

The next three scenes were mini scenes of checking the roads into the three areas with cuts back to the map and showing where the roads went. One check panned on the entrance to a campground and then the road that went past it up the mountain to Matanuska Glacier State lookout point. Ignirtoq pointed to the car tracks and said that he bet that they would find Grayson when they went to where the road ended. The view of the snow covered surrounding with the green of the pines breaking the brilliant white of the snow reflecting the sun and the wind blowing the dry snow between the pine seemed to cast a spell that caused everyone to hold their breath.

Ignirtoq commented that he was going to continue taking pictures, but he was no longer going to talk because he knew that somewhere close ahead, he was sure that Grayson would be sitting in his tent or at a campfire. The camera caught Clay going from tree to tree and Ignirtoq doing the same.

Then the camera caught Grayson sitting in his tent, raising his rifle, and looking through the scope. The screen went blank, but the sound captured the sound of a bullet hitting something close to it and then the close at hand sound of a shot being fired. The sound of another rifle close to where Ignirtoq was located could be heard and then Clay shouting that he would provide cover, but he needed Ignirtoq to take Grayson out.

Ignirtoq could be heard saying he was going to take Trey's advice, step out, fire from the hip, and then fall to the ground and take the kill shot. The sequence was caught in sound and with Clay shouting that he would provide cover. Ignirtoq's two subsequent shots could be heard and then the camera came back on and Ignirtoq could be heard quietly saying that he thought that it had worked, and the shoulder wound didn't hurt too much.

After a moment, Ignirtoq stood up and the camera captured his slow, cautious walk toward the camp. Then Grayson's body was in the center of the screen and a dark pool of blood could be seen in the snow.

The camera turned and took in the surrounding panoramic view. The next scene was of an approaching helicopter, its landing and the paramedics and police getting out of the helicopter.

Clay could be heard asking if Ignirtoq would be OK.

The camera seemed to change hands and the scene was Ignirtoq being treated for a bullet wound in the shoulder and then getting air lifted out by helicopter.

The camera caught a flurry of police arriving up the trail.

Then it went blank and came on with the scene of Ignirtoq sitting in a hospital bed with Atiqtalik and Kaskae on each side of the bed.

Ignirtoq smiled and said that his lesson from Trey on how to take out the enemy had worked but Trey had failed to warn him that he could also get shot.

Northern Lights

The video ended with, "The good guys won and lived happily ever after."

There were cheers from everyone listening and congratulations on effectively closing the case.

The Chief added if he got a copy of the video, he would not need a written closing report and added that he was now ready for the main barbeque course of Brats and Wursts.

The End

Ron Mueller

Northern Lights

<u>**About the Author**</u>

Ronald E. Mueller
remwriter95@gmail.com

Ron grew up in what is now Flint River State Park in Southeast Iowa. The 170-year-old house Ron lived in is built into a hillside. It faces a 125-foot-high cliff towering over the little Flint River. The house and the land talked to him about; the passing of time, the struggle to conquer the land, the struggles people faced and the wonder of nature.

He climbed the cliffs, crawled into the caves, dove from the swimming rock, collected clams from the bottom of the pond, gigged and skinned frogs for their legs. He trapped muskrats for fur, hunted raccoon in the dead of night, and with only a stick hunted rabbits in the dead of winter.

His young life was outdoors, and nature tested him.

He walked to a one room stone schoolhouse uphill both ways. A stern but warm-hearted teacher, Mrs. Henry was instrumental in shaping his character as she shepherded him from the fourth to the eighth grade. A Montessori before its time. It was a great way to grow up.

His experiences inter-twined with snippets of fantasy lend themselves to the adventures he leads the reader through.

Ron Mueller

Northern Lights

<u>Characters in the Story</u>

Alex	Cathy	Evercrest	Police Detective
Matthew	Timothy	Knolton	Alex's suitor
Rose-Anne	Germain	Evercrest	Alex's mother
Russel	Johnson	Evercrest	Alex's father
Helping Hands charity			Alex's nonprofit org
Trey		McGregor	Alex's Detective Partner
Lindsey		McGregor	Wife
Nolan		McGregor	Son
Johnnie		Smith	Old Viet Vet
Mary		Higgins	Johnnie's Phili "friend"
Bruce	Lincoln	Johnson	Cinci Chief of Detectives
Mary-Anne	Leslie	Johnson	Chiefs Wife
Bill	Hamilton	Danson	Detective
Travis	Bailey	Carter	Detective
Dr. Rogers			Coroner
Jane	Elousie	Stradford	Lieutenant Governor
Felix			proprietor at fishing dock
Golden Goose			Name of the Yacht
Sandra		Olson	Policewoman guard
Annie	Lorie	Scots	Missing girl
Linda		Annies	older daughter
Lorie		Annies	second daughter
Harold		Zimmerman	Chicago DEA
James	Oscor	Kaizer	Sheriff of Wiggin
Abbie	Alisa	Bender	married James
John	S.	Williams	Lawyer was abused
Hanna		Waverly	John's mate
Angelica			Angel on the hill
Brian		Lexter	FBI Bureau Chief
Cais		Leu	Alex's Viet friend
Tracy		Hunter	Trey's Analyst

<u>Northern Lights</u>

Ignirtoq			Inuit who discovers someone stealing
Atiqtalik			Local Forest Ranger
Kaskae			Son of Ignirtoq
Grayson		Gagnon	Oil Thief
Myles		Walker	Buyer of the Oil
Clay			Bush Pilot
Reginald		Sailor	RCMP Chief
Delia		Tislen	RCMP field leader

Ron Mueller

Published by: Around the World Publishing LLC.

QR Links to

ATWP.US web site

www.ingramcontent.com/pod-product-compliance
Lightning Source LLC
Chambersburg PA
CBHW060556100726
47907CB00005B/1388